MELISSA SMITH

WHAT I DIDN'T DO

A BAR HARBOR PSYCHOLOGICAL THRILLER

Copyright © February 29, 2024 by Melissa Smith

All rights reserved.

No portion of this book may be reproduced in any form without written permission from the publisher or author, except as permitted by U.S. copyright law.

Contents

1. One — 1
2. Two — 28
3. Three — 41
4. Four — 52
5. Five — 70
6. Six — 88
7. Seven — 102
8. Eight — 124
9. Nine — 142
10. Ten — 155
11. MORE BY MELISSA — 176

ONE

Clouds stretched out below me like foggy rivers, long wispy fingers meandering this way and that, much like my thoughts. It was true I'd failed meteorology in college. I'd taken it as an elective science, to make myself look well-rounded and ambitious. Now I silently wished I'd paid more attention. I knew the billowing clouds were steaming off the streams beneath them, but from my altitude, it looked magical. Mesmerizing, even. It was enchanting to watch the rolling landscape from above. The wind rippled over the lakes and ponds. The sun glistened on the water; the grays and blues and greens transformed into a light so bright you struggled not to look away. How sad, I thought, to be blind and never see such beauty.

"Why does it do that?" I nudged my husband and motioned out the tiny window.

"What?" He could barely hear me. My voice was soft, just over a murmur, but I felt like I was yelling.

"The clouds," I spoke louder and pointed out the window. "How do they do that?"

He shrugged and returned his attention to his solitaire game, clearly uninterested in cloud formations. I couldn't stop thinking about the clouds. The fluffy, snow-colored, wondrous cotton balls adorned the bright blue sky around me and I wondered, was he out there somewhere, right this moment, missing me? Was he thinking about me, staring at the clouds like a love-struck assassin?

I'd like to say it's been years since I thought of him. Of his touch, his smile, his subtle gentilities. The truth of it is not so direct. I miss him. I miss our adventures. I miss his cues, the way we could read each other. I miss studying him for hours on end. Most of all, I miss our silent connection. I could look into his eyes and know from his expression whether I should move my head a bit to the left or right, to avoid his bullets. I would get off on the feeling of blood splattering on my neck and face after he pulled the trigger. He and I were magical, just like these clouds.

I was seventeen years old when I first met Henry. He was thirty-seven. I graduated early from high school, the result of a mundane life. I was smart, graduating first in my class of almost two hundred peers. I was beautiful, a knock-out some would say with my extra-long legs and tan olive complexion. My dark brown eyes took in the world around me, anxious to leave my current life in the dust. I could do anything I wanted, go anywhere I wanted, and become anyone I wanted to be, but I wanted nothing.

I grew up in the ever-popular tourist trap of Bar Harbor. What used to be a quaint fishing village on the east coast of Maine had, over the years, transformed into an oasis of lost girls. No one noticed at first; there were so many vacationers. Maine is known for its rustic coastline. Rocky hiking trails, blueberry patches, and of course lobsters are but a few of Maine's treasures. I didn't enjoy hiking or blueberries or lobsters for that matter, but many families would plan their summers around their annual trips to indulge in these simple treats. Generation-owned bed and breakfasts scattered across the countryside, decorating the cliffs like beacons of warmth and comfort.

Once in a while, tragedies couldn't be avoided. I'll never forget the story of Emily, a girl barely twelve years old whose family was visiting Acadia from New York City. New Yorkers loved to visit Maine in August when the stifling city heat became almost unbearable. Emily's family always stayed at Ocean's Edge, where the seals could be seen sunning themselves on the warm rocks at low tide. One day, Emily and her parents along with her two little brothers, ages five and seven, rented bicycles and pedaled their way through the infamous national park. Their mother packed a picnic lunch provided by the kitchen staff at the B&B. They sat together at one of the many picnic tables along the parkway, enjoying the sunshine and fried chicken. The tranquility of nature soaked into them, breeding a peaceful state of mind incomparable to anything New York could offer.

When they continued on the bike trail after finishing their lunch, they had no worries, not a care in the world, until Emily's little brother had to stop to tie his shoelace. Emily, being the oldest, had ridden faster than the others and didn't hear her father call to her to stop and wait for them. She peddled on, around the bend in the road ahead and disappeared, never to be seen again. Her, or her pale yellow banana seat bicycle.

Then there was Jessica, who, as the story goes, slipped on a wet rock while watching the sun come up on the misty horizon. Acadia National Park's Cadillac Mountain is the first place in the United States where the sun kisses the sky every morning. It's not uncommon for visitors to arise before dawn and travel up the steep mountain road to take in the breathtaking sunrises. Jessica hadn't been alone. At the age of fourteen, she'd also been traveling with her family, but no one saw her slip and tumble down the cliff. No one heard her screams. And no one found her body, undoubtedly shattered on the rocks. Police and rescue personnel searched for days to no avail.

These were but two of the horrific tales I'd heard. There were more, many, many more, but until I met Henry, I didn't realize the complexities and similarities of the countless disappearances. Growing up I'd always assumed they were fables, twisted tales of kidnappings and murders meant to scare young minds into obedience. Stay close to your parents. Never wander off. Do not run away or else you may never be seen again. Gone, forever!

I've known life outside Bar Harbor. My parents, both business executives, were constantly traveling. My fascination with clouds started at a very young age. I don't remember most of our trips, maybe they blur together, but I always remember the feeling of joy I felt when arriving at home. Vacations were nice but it was always awkward being around my parents. Home was better because I could be alone. I was alone at a very young age and always so after I became a teenager. I never asked my parents for specifics about their jobs. They were strangers to me. I was never sure if I was an unfortunate mistake for them or if they were missing the parent gene. Either way, I became very good at taking care of myself. They left me credit cards and I lived on grocery deliveries until I got my license. When I turned sixteen, they bought me a car, a steel gray Mustang, because nothing screams 'I love you' like a car dropped off with a note like a bouquet of roses.

"Perfect by nature, I come from self-indulgence..." The wrong lyrics of my favorite Evanescence song summed up my existence. And I was perfect. I shined academically. Socially, I had friends when I wanted them, but I preferred to be alone. Alone was comfortable. Henry changed all that when we met. He tipped my world upside down, shaking me like a stuck snow globe. It was almost as if he wiped my slate clean and completely reeducated me. He performed a factory reset on me and I never questioned anything about it. I needed it. Henry brought me back to life.

I am not a woman who values old-fashioned traditions. I could do away with most holidays. My husband is the one who decorates for Christmas. I assume it's because of our different upbringings. Derek had a safe, happy, regular childhood. He played tee ball and soccer and took karate lessons. He had parents and grandparents and aunts and uncles. Derek's childhood could have been pictured in any home magazine. His mind was clogged with cheerful Christmas memories. He couldn't possibly fathom not celebrating it. I played along only for his enjoyment. I burned Christmas-scented candles and filled glass Christmas tree jars full of Christmas candy. Red, green, silver, and gold were all beautiful colors, but they held no emotions for me. I tolerated Christmas but I wasn't going overboard and making fudge or handmade ornaments that we could paint and cherish forever. That wasn't me. Derek knew this, so he took control. It was a decent arrangement, I thought.

The reality of the situation was that Christmas was when I met Henry. It was the first Christmas after my high school graduation. I was home alone, per usual. My parents could have been in Europe or California, I had no idea. That Christmas Eve was especially lonely for some reason. It was not the first time I'd been solo on this day but for some reason today, I was left with a haunting feeling of darkness that I couldn't shake no matter how hard I tried. The day was almost over when I decided to venture out and buy a tree. A fake, small, tabletop tree was all I wanted. I wasn't sure why I wanted one, but I remember the dark loneliness being incredibly palpable. I could reach out and touch it. I could poke it. I could feel it beating with the rhythm of my own heart. Maybe it was because most of my friendships had dissipated after graduation. I missed human connections. I had been accepted into Boston University but I had no interest in actually attending. I knew I needed to make a plan. I didn't want to stay here forever. Valedictorian at seventeen years old, I still had no idea where to start or how to approach anyone for help. I had been given a full ride to BU and didn't go. What kind of idiot does that?

It was a crisp cool December afternoon. I walked down Main Street, oblivious to my surroundings as I peeked in storefront windows in search of a small tree. When I turned away from the third shop window where I'd been staring at a toy train, I bumped squarely into him. His gray goatee made him look distinguished, important somehow, like he should be wearing a fancy tailored suit with a wool dress coat draped around his shoulders and a designer scarf wrapped around his neck. Instead, he wore blue jeans and a tan Carhartt jacket.

"I'm sorry," I stuttered.

"Don't be," he replied.

We stared at each other for what felt like a very long time.

"I'm Henry." He introduced himself and held his hand out to shake mine. His hand felt strong even through my soft winter driving glove.

"I'm Ryan," I smiled at him as I let my brain recognize how handsome he was. Older, yes, but he had an air about him that felt of adventure and danger. I let my hand linger in his. The hairs on the back of my neck sizzled. I swallowed hard and dropped my hand to my side.

"Window shopping?" Henry asked. His full smile let me peek at his perfect white teeth.

"Sort of," I laughed. "I'm looking for a tree."

"You know Christmas is tomorrow?" He teased me.

"Yes," I blushed. "It's last minute for sure!"

"There's a tree shop on the right, almost to the end," he pointed down the street toward the water. "I can show you if you'd like." His blue eyes twinkled to match the string lights hanging in the storefront window and I was helpless to resist.

"Ryan is a unique name for a lady," he commented as we walked down the hill.

"Yes it is," I acknowledged with a nod. "I like it. It's original."

"It's beautiful," he insisted. "Hey, if I may be so bold, would you like to grab a coffee before your big tree purchase? There's a cafe right up here that makes delicious warm drinks."

I didn't look at him as I agreed, probably too quickly. I blamed the cold breeze coming off the ocean. I sensed him smiling as he led the way to the cafe. He held the door open for me like a true gentleman and we sat down at the bar. The place had a flat, dark appearance like it was trying too hard to be modern, but it smelled of coffee beans and freshly baked sweets. The waitress came over and started jabbering away, telling us the specials of the day, only to be interrupted by my new friend.

"We'd like two Christmas cookie hot chocolates, please," he ordered stiffly.

I wondered for a moment if my mind was playing tricks on me. The waitress scurried off and Henry turned to look at me. We were sitting very close together, our swiveling bar stools allowing our knees to touch. Adrenaline coursed through my body, reminding me how new and exciting this was. It was as if this were my first human connection in decades.

"Wait, Ryan? Ryan..." he clicked his tongue like he was trying to recall important information. "You graduated first in your class this year, right?"

"Yup," I giggled. "That's me."

"That is quite a feat! Congratulations!" He was clearly impressed.

"Thank you," I said quietly as the waitress placed two round mugs of hot cocoa in front of us. They were topped with whipped cream and sprinkles. A thin sugar cookie peeked out from the side of the foamy topping.

"This looks amazing!" I beamed.

"Enjoy!" he said. I watched him slurp his cocoa and when he looked at me again whipped cream covered his upper lip and mustache. Without thinking, I reached over and wiped his lip clean with my index finger. Then I slowly licked my finger, my eyes never leaving his. Something stirred inside me, a hunger that had been sleeping until now, hibernating within me.

"Do you want to get out of here?" I whispered.

"Yes." His eyes fondled every inch of me. He laid a twenty dollar bill down on the bar and we made our way out of the crowded cafe, my drink completely untouched.

We walked down toward the pier, bypassing the tree shop as we went. We stopped at a park bench just barely out of reach of the streetlight. He sat down and I stood in front of him. His sandy blonde hair was trying to turn gray under his Red Stripe baseball cap. His face was shadowed by the distant light. I could feel his stare singeing my skin even through my ski jacket.

"I'm old enough to be your father," he shifted slightly on the bench. I stepped closer to him and draped my right leg around his waist, then my left.

"Are you?" I straddled him as I spoke. My voice sounded husky to my ears. "Are you my father?"

"I am not." He sighed heavily. I could feel his breathing quickening. I placed his sweaty palms on my jeans. My thighs were hot under the fabric. I silently wondered if he could feel the heat as well.

"How old are you, exactly?" He inquired hesitantly.

"I'll be eighteen next week," I answered. "How old are you?"

"I'm thirty-seven," he gripped my thighs tighter.

"Twenty years," I unzipped my jacket.

"Twenty years," he repeated. He shifted himself again.

"Am I...am I making you uncomfortable?" I asked innocently. "Would you rather wait until next week when I magically transform into an adult?"

I sat back on his legs and noticed his erection was winning any moral argument his brain was trying to conquer.

"Listen," I laughed. "Honestly, I'm just enjoying your company. I'm never like this. It must be something in the air." I twirled my hair with one finger, my nervous trademark.

"I want you, obviously," he chuckled half-heartedly. "I just don't want you to think I'm one of those creepy old men."

"Apparently I like creepy old men," I teased.

"Let's go buy your tree and see where the night takes us," he gently set me on the bench next to him.

I quickly gathered my wits about me, embarrassed by my forwardness. We walked back up the short hill to the tree shop. The trees out front were all gone so we went inside. It was an old mercantile, complete with an antique smell of old wood and furniture polish. We asked the clerk who was sweeping the floor if there were any more trees and he shook his head no. As we turned to leave a small tabletop lamp in the storefront window caught my eye. It was brass with curvy metal arms that stretched out like tree branches. Someone had hung a few green Christmas bulbs on it, giving it a festive yet quaint feel.

"That's what I want!" I clapped my hands together like an excited child then quickly stopped when I remembered I wasn't alone.

"That's not a Christmas tree," Henry looked at me quizzically.

"Sure it is!" I argued. "And I can leave it out all year long." I unplugged the lamp, picked it up off the table, and brought it to the counter.

"Oh honey, that's not for sale," The old lady behind the register set the lamp to the side.

"Please," I begged. "I love it! I'll pay anything."

"Well, I guess…" The woman rubbed her forehead incredulously.

"How much?" I grinned and held my wallet out, ready to throw my money at her.

"Twenty dollars, I guess," the woman grunted.

I tossed a hundred-dollar bill on the counter and quickly snatched up my new lamp. The glass balls chimed together joyfully as we marched out of the shop.

"You know you gave her one hundred dollars, right?" Henry hurried to catch up with me.

"Yeah, I know." My cheeks felt cold and rosy as I spoke. "I guess I got struck by the Christmas spirit."

"That's very generous of you," Henry approved.

"I love this!" I held the lamp tighter. "Plus, I didn't want her to change her mind!"

Henry walked beside me as I made my way back to my car. He was quiet with a brooding expression on his face. I had parked in one of the last available slots on the busy street. Our tiny city was abustle with last-minute shoppers. Some appeared irritated by the chaotic holiday, while others looked like they were bathed in the magic of the season. Gleeful with pure, rare ambiance; a happiness that can't be measured. Children to the right of us were sticking their tongues out to catch the glistening snowflakes that danced softly in the darkening sky. A middle-aged couple scurried past us, their arms loaded to the max with bags. An elderly couple sat on a park bench, snuggled together with a blanket, drinking from a thermos and watching the world around them. Henry remained quiet beside me and I desperately wanted to know what he was thinking.

"I'm sorry about all that, back there at the bench," I said as I stopped at my car. "I honestly don't know what came over me." I set my lamp gently in the back seat.

"It was nice to meet you, Ryan." Henry reached for my hand and held it up to his lips. He kissed my knuckles tenderly before turning and walking away. I watched him walk, my eyes glued to his back. It was an image I was used to seeing, men walking away. Mostly just my dad. Broad shoulders in the distance were as serene an image as a child crying on the sidewalk. Something you hated to see, something that reminded you of your own humanity. I let my eyes fall to the ground, then

I glanced in my car at my newfound treasure. I smiled and let out a long sigh.

I got in my car and drove home. I didn't know what to think of Henry. He was chivalrous, yet edgy. Older yes, but I'd never been interested in guys my own age. I had an older spirit than my peers. Unaccustomed to parties or even malls, I didn't fit in with the usual crowd. It was something I'd learned to embrace. I liked libraries, cafes, gardens, and apparently lamps.

When I arrived home, I pulled my car up to the garage door and parked. I didn't like parking inside the garage. Truth be told, I didn't like to back out. I trudged through the few inches of fresh snow to my breezeway door. We had an older, colonial-style home, built in the 1930's, but recently remodeled. White with black shutters, super original. The garage, complete with a paved driveway was to the right, then the breezeway, then the house on the left. A white picket fence enclosed the entire property, even stretching out back to the patio and inground pool. It was a beautiful place, just a few miles south of town.

I walked into the kitchen and set my new lamp down on the dark green granite countertop. I plugged it in and pulled a bar stool over so I could sit in front of it. I rolled the dial on the cord between my fingers until it clicked on. I sat with my cheeks resting in my hands as I stared at the soft golden glow and glimmered green bulbs.

"Merry Christmas, Ryan," I whispered into the empty house.

I sat and stared for over an hour as sadness threatened to overwhelm me. I was sad to be home alone, sad to not be wanted, sad to have no one to love. Suddenly, the doorbell rang, thankfully snapping me out of my sappy mood. I opened the heavy oak door and there he was, Henry, holding two bags of Chinese take-out and a real Christmas tree.

"I hope it's okay I'm here," the look in his eyes begged for acceptance.

"It is!" I exclaimed happily.

I took the bags from him so he could carry the tree inside. It was a Charlie Brown sort of tree, maybe three feet tall. He asked me to hold the tree for a minute while he ran back outside. When he returned, he had a small tote of lights and decorations, even a tree stand. He proceeded to set it up on top of my dining room table. I watched him from the kitchen as I grabbed plates and forks. He draped a string of colored lights around the frail tree and smiled at me, clearly very proud of his thoughtful accomplishment. We sat down at the end of the massive table and watched the lights dance on the tree while we ate.

"Have you never celebrated Christmas?" he asked.

"I don't think so," I shook my head, oblivious to any memories associated with jolly old St. Nick. "My parents are rarely home. They are always away on business."

"So, you're here alone most of the time?" He seemed more concerned than intrigued.

"Yeah," I shrugged. "I pretty much raised myself but like I said, I'll be eighteen next week. I'm ready to be officially on my own." I knew I'd never be completely on my own. Richard and Diane would continue to send me money until their dying day and probably after. Guilt money, I suppose. Guilt money for the daughter they didn't love.

"That sounds like a very lonely life." Henry looked at me over his plate of beef and broccoli.

"Yeah," I cleared my throat and looked down at my plate. "I suppose that's partly why I acted so...um, aggressively earlier. I can be socially awkward."

"Honey, that's not awkwardness," Henry gazed at me intensely.

I knew he was right. It wasn't awkwardness I'd felt on the park bench or in the cafe. It was desire and it made me breathe heavily even now, just thinking about it.

As we continued eating, I watched Henry and I wondered what demons had entangled his soul. Why was he thirty-seven and single? Was he single? I guess I never asked. What was his story? Why didn't he have anywhere else to be on Christmas Eve? Was he lonely too? Questions swirled in my mind.

"I lost my family last year," he sat back in his chair as he spoke. His words caught me off guard, like a sail snapping in the stiff ocean breeze. "My daughter was six," the sail snapped again.

"I'm so sorry, Henry. I can't imagine." I looked from him to his half-full plate of food and waited for him to continue. When he didn't, I softly pressed him for more information. "How?" my voice was barely audible.

"I have to confess something," he pushed his plate back and rested his hands on the table. "Our meeting today wasn't by chance. It wasn't a coincidence or fate. I've been watching you for quite some time. Please, don't be scared. I'm not a bad person."

"I'm listening," I swallowed.

He had my full attention now. His square jaw trembled, drawing me in. As hard as I tried, I couldn't look away.

"Ryan, what I am about to tell you is going to sound ludicrous I know, but please hear me out." He slid a manila folder toward me. "In this file, you'll find over twenty missing girls, ranging from as young as my Suzie to right around your age. My Suzie was taken from me in a car heist. I was coming out of the market and saw the whole thing happen. A masked man shot my wife and pushed her body out the passenger door. I always thought it was odd that he kept Suzie. Maybe he didn't know she was there at first. Maybe she was hiding on the floor after watching her mom get shot. After weeks of no leads and empty searches, I started researching missing people in the area, specifically Bar Harbor, and the results were sickening. It's shocking and appalling to me how over twenty missing girls can go unnoticed." He stopped talking and raked his fingers through his hair. "I'm sorry to ambush you with all of this Ryan but, I desperately need your help."

I could tell he was being sincere. He was fraught with worry, antsy with what I assumed was anger or anxiety, probably both. I let my eyes drop to the file in front of my plate.

"I apologize for coming at you with all of this tonight, I just...well, to be honest, I thought you were eighteen. You graduated in June and I just assumed. I haven't seen you out and about for a while so when I saw you today I just had to approach you."

"How long have you been watching me?" I whispered the question, making myself sound smaller than anticipated.

"Since my wife's death and my daughter's disappearance."

"How did you know me?" I was skeptical.

"You were on a list of people we'd just interviewed for babysitting. I remembered you because..." he stopped.

"Because why?" I sat up taller in my chair. "Because you were so beautiful," he admitted shyly. "Anyway, yes, I've been watching you. For one thing, you look older than you are. And another thing, I noticed, in my stalking of you, is that you are alone almost all of the time. Occasionally you'll walk with a friend or go to a movie with a group, but nine out of ten times, you are alone."

I didn't say anything. He was right. The thought of him watching me was arousing in ways I'd never felt until now. I couldn't even pretend to be upset.

"I thought maybe you'd be interested in a project," he cleared his voice, his eyes pleading with mine.

"What kind of project?" I was intrigued. I knew I was alone too much. That was the whole reason for my little tree-shopping excursion earlier tonight.

"I'm going to find this asshole, whoever's been stealing all these girls, if it's the last thing I do. I'll get my little girl back or I'll die trying." His face was red as he fought back unbidden tears. "Will you just look over this file and let me know what you think?"

"Of course," I nodded. I didn't know what else to say. I watched as he stood up. His shoulders were more slumped than before like someone had drained all the air out of him. Like he was terrified I'd say no, or that I'd think he was crazy. He walked to the door and turned back to look at me. Sensing his apprehension, I tossed my cloth napkin on the table and met him in the doorway. He looked down at me as if he were staring at a slot machine, desperately hoping to get the jackpot. Maybe he'd never experienced luck. Maybe he thought I would be his luck. Either way, I took his hand in mine and squeezed it reassuringly.

"I'll look at it right now. Do you have a number I can reach you at?" I tried to sound hopeful yet realistic.

"I'll be at the park bench tomorrow at noon," he cleared his throat.

"Tomorrow's Christmas..." I started to object and stopped when I realized how lonely he must be without his family. "I'd love to see you on Christmas!" I smiled up at him.

"If you're interested, meet me there. If not, Merry Christmas!" he shrugged quickly.

"Thank you for trusting me with this," I squeezed his hand again. "And thank you for saying I'm beautiful."

He leaned down and kissed my cheek softly and I wondered if my skin burnt his lips.

Two

I never experienced heartbreak before Henry. As a child, I never knew the stinging blow of a parent missing an event or holiday. I never knew parents were required to attend. In my world, parents were breadwinners. They gave me life and provided me with everything I needed to navigate it. They weren't around to be spectators. They were too busy with all the bread. Their absence was not negative or positive, it just was.

I never knew the heartache of a family member dying because, in reality, I had no family. I had a nanny, Miss Jenny, when I was young. She cooked and cleaned and transported me wherever I needed to go. She shopped for me and read me stories. She came to my science fair and tee ball games.

Her employment was terminated when I turned thirteen because teenagers should be self-sufficient and I was, for the most part. If there was something I was unsure about, I figured it out pretty quickly with the internet.

As I grew, I never had relationships because I didn't allow myself any free time. My daily schedule was packed with school and homework, as well as trying to maintain a clean house with a stocked refrigerator. It was a lot for a teenager to care for alone, but not only did I manage, I excelled at it. There were times when I loved my freedom. Other times, I felt strangled by it.

The contract I read when I turned thirteen, AKA my birthday card, clearly stated that now, as a teenager, I was responsible for taking care of myself. That included keeping out of trouble, making excellent grades a priority, and living a life free of the stench of impropriety, to the extent that it had to appear as though I didn't live alone. As long as I kept my end of the bargain, I had a beautiful house to live in, a spending account for groceries, and a credit card for anything I may need or want. When I turned sixteen I would get a car as long as our contract remained unbreeched. When I turned eighteen, I had the choice of moving out or staying, either way, I'd still have my spending account and credit card. If I moved out, they would pay for my new place.

The road was neatly paved in front of me. Yellow-lined black tar stretched as far as the eye could see. Until I met Henry I never thought to navigate off the path. Why would I? I had everything I needed at my fingertips. It was true, I struggled after graduation. I missed human contact. I had no direction. I felt no real meaning in my life. I suppose that's what happens when you dedicate all your time to school and then in one ceremony it's finished, thrusting you into your next chapter whether you're ready for it or not. I had never even had a part-time job. I didn't need one. I had zero real-life experiences. I certainly didn't worry about my loved ones vanishing.

Now, as I sat at my table staring into the glow of my new lamp, I wondered if this modern, easy life was what I really wanted. I could live a comfortable life here. I could work at any of the little shops in town. I could sell antiques or lobster traps or bake cupcakes if I wanted to. Hell, I could stay at home every day and do nothing and all of my expenses would still be paid in full. Maybe I would meet my soulmate at the pottery studio on a Wednesday night while I crafted lawn ornaments. Or maybe I'd meet him while window shopping on Christmas Eve and I'd ravenously throw myself at him on a park bench. Images of our time on the park bench flooded my mind, stirring me from my trance. I looked from the glistening light to the ominous folder still untouched on the table. I thought of Henry's soft eyes as he told me about his dead wife and missing child.

"We weren't meant to live alone," I whispered into the light.

Henry's sadness took my breath away. He had experienced deep unbridled loss. At that moment I realized how many feelings I was missing out on, stuck here all by myself. Maybe I was socially awkward, or sexually awkward rather. Maybe I jumped the gun by straddling him on the park bench.

Maybe I shouldn't have done that, but maybe, just maybe, it was the first step on my own path to a more invigorating life.

I stood up and walked to the coffee bar that was nestled into the wall under the staircase. The house was gorgeously decorated, which I took credit for even though Diane had hired a professional design team. The floor plan flowed nicely throughout the downstairs. The front door opened into a small pale yellow foyer. There was a closet for hanging coats, an umbrella stand, and a high-back cream-colored chair that I could remember sitting in when Miss Jenny taught me how to tie my shoes. To the left of the foyer was the kitchen, with light gray walls and windows trimmed with thick white grooved frames. No curtains, only blinds, with big billowy dark gray valances atop the windows. The kitchen cupboards were all white with skinny, steel-colored knobs. The appliances were, of course, stainless steel. A chrome KitchenAid mixer sat on the dark green granite countertop next to a family-sized, four-slice toaster, which I always thought was overkill because a family did not live here. A large island took up most of the space in the center of the room. A small sink sunk inside the island, situated to the right of a six-burner stove. Again, overkill. Two ovens were in the wall directly behind the stove. Four white bar stools lined up neatly next to the back side of the island. A high-capacity dishwasher and larger kitchen sink were tucked along the back wall, next to a side door that led to the fenced-in yard. I spent most of my time in the kitchen. Its large windows let in a ton of natural light and, although this room never heard voices of a happy family, it heard me talking to myself quite a lot, or singing along to Alexa, or cursing over my latest burnt creation.

Straight through the foyer and to the right was the living room. To the left was a study, which I rarely went into. Leather couches, hardwood floors, and expensive paintings decorated these rooms like they were waiting patiently for important guests, or the governor even, to come sit and sip gin. I wanted to put carpet in the living room, wall to wall, thick bright blue carpet, or maybe lavender. Carpet you could lay on comfortably while watching old home videos. I recognized this was but a pipe dream. Diane would never allow carpet. We didn't have home videos anyway, or a home for that matter. To the right of the foyer was the dining room, equipped with a coffee station, and massive dark oak table, and matching chairs. This room had gray walls also, but curtains to match the billowy valances that adorned the windows. A chandelier hung from the ceiling, centered perfectly over the table. Usually, this room was unused, but tonight it looked warm and inviting thanks to Henry's Christmas tree.

I started a pot of my favorite dark roast coffee. I leaned against the wall as I waited for the coffee to brew and I stared at the mysterious folder. I knew I would open it. What I didn't know was why this smothering uncomfortable feeling kept creeping up my spine and falling over my shoulders, only to trail slowly down my torso and settle at the moist spot between my legs. I knew I wanted more than this carefully calculated life I was leading. This feeling of excitement, teetering with desire and uncertainty, was the sweetest feeling in the world.

I put two sugars in my coffee and a healthy dose of cream. I stirred it, getting lost in the caramel swirls, and sipped it slowly before mustering up all the courage I could find and walking to the dining room table. I sat down and slid the file closer to myself. I knew I was already past the point of no return.

I opened the file and laid it flat in front of me. Suzie's picture was paperclipped to the first page. She was sitting on a little orange chair, smiling big for the camera. It looked very much like a kindergarten picture, or maybe first grade. Her red curls landed just above her shoulders. Her pretty pink dress was accompanied by pretty pink sneakers. I looked at the shoes, they looked like the same light-up ones I had when I was a kid. I loved those shoes! Miss Jenny had bought them for me, I remembered with a smile. Suzie's blue eyes looked happy, way happier than my eyes looked in any of my school pictures. I peeled the photo up enough to read the inscription on the back. *Suzie, 6 years old.*

Attached to Suzie's picture was a detailed police report depicting the events of the day. The day Henry's world changed forever. The police report was followed by Henry's wife Catherine's death certificate. I sat there humbled, my own life suddenly feeling very irrelevant. Pages and pages of missing girls, their eyes digging deep into mine. My fingers stopped working when I saw Molly's image staring back at me. Molly had been in my homeroom at school. We were all told she'd moved away. Why would they lie to us? Why not tell the truth, that she disappeared? Did they not want us to be vigilant and aware? Shouldn't we have known? Beyond that, just how deep did this go? I thought of my teacher, my respected homeroom teacher, telling us with zero emotion that Molly had moved away. I was friends with Molly, not super close, but friends nonetheless, and now as I stared at her image, I thought surely she would have told me if she were going to move away.

Molly, Jessica, Emily, Suzie, and all the others were all taken abruptly, innocently, their lives ravaged, their bodies stolen. Tears fell down my cheeks. Try as I might, I couldn't help but cry over the fear and devastation Suzie must have been feeling. To have her mother shot in front of her, to watch her body get dumped into the street. My heart shattered for Suzie, for Henry.

I pushed the papers toward the middle of the long rectangular table. This table rarely saw more than two guests. In fact, I could count on one hand the times it had been set for a family of three. Occasionally I'd have a friend over and we'd do homework at it. This table had seen more science experiments and poster projects than it had satisfied tummies. I sat back in my chair, slouching, heavy with the weight of my new knowledge. A haunting thought smothered me. Why was I spared? I'd been living alone for almost five years. The premium age, it seemed, to be kidnapped. If this was happening all around me, why was I still here? What made my life more valuable, or less so, than Jessica and Emily and Molly? Why would they take a six-year-old child like Suzie, but leave me alone?

I shivered, my skin prickling. I glanced over at the corner hutch that housed our fancy china. China we had never used. China and a single-family portrait. It was a five-by-seven image, far be it for them to splurge and get a big one. I was eleven in the picture, standing proudly between my two parents. They each had an arm around my shoulders. The perfect family photo. A portrait of strangers I didn't know. I couldn't remember why the picture had been taken, but I remember feeling a sense of happiness with their arms around me. Now here I sat, a few feet away from the photo, wondering if everything I knew in my life was going to suddenly flip upside down. Was I spared because they were the masterminds behind this madness? Did my parents steal little girls, murdering anyone in their way? Why? Did my mother keep my father away from me on purpose? To keep me safe from his animalistic urges?

I got up and poured myself another cup of coffee. My mind raced, spinning uncontrollably. I wished Henry hadn't left. I wished he'd stayed. To hand me this information and leave, on Christmas Eve, was rather rude. Now I was trapped on this hamster wheel, unable to calm the tormentous spinning. I knew in my gut that my parents were involved. How could they not be? It must be why they stayed away, why they supplied me with money, why they never loved me at all. I was a mistake, now a business transaction. Nothing more than a write-off.

I walked back over to the table and spread out all the images. I studied them. Several of the missing girls had been here on vacation. Most of them had attached incident reports, like Jessica, who had presumably fallen off the cliffs of Cadillac Mountain, and Trina, who had supposedly been crushed to death at Thunder Hole. The waves were powerful there, they could easily drown someone, but the report had said 'crushed to death' and, again, no body found. There was a grueling bear attack, heard but not seen, a suicide, a parasailing accident, as well as several reports of girls out jogging, never to return home. I had been jogging, walking, and running more times than I could remember. All alone. I'd never seen anything suspicious or felt unsafe. I'd never known the fright of abduction. I could barely fathom it.

The wee morning hours arrived and I was still mesmerized by the contents of the folder. I'd consumed a whole pot of coffee and I knew there was no way I could wait until noon to see Henry. I stacked the pages back inside the folder and put the folder in my backpack. I slipped into my winter boots and jacket and stepped out into the fresh Christmas air.

Three

A screaming child from the front of the plane brought me back to the here and now. I shook my head and pinched the bridge of my slender nose. My sinuses were congested, my ears plugged. My body hated flying even though my mind loved it. Flying was a natural high, no pun intended. The pilot's voice came across the speakers. We were beginning our initial descent into New Jersey. Newark, yuck. Nothing was appealing about Newark. The airport, or the city. Shipping containers as far as the eye could see made for a revolting landscape. My heart sank every time I saw a shipping container, even now, more than two decades later.

Derek and I never had children. Babies were not in the cards. Well, maybe they were, but not in the deck we played with. The truth was, after Henry, after all the things we saw and did, I never wanted kids. The world is too evil for kids. I knew if I ever reproduced I'd never have a peaceful moment again. My mind wouldn't allow me sanity. I couldn't have a baby and watch it grow and ever let it leave my sight. My children would grow into teenagers who despised me. Their house would be a prison, much like mine was. Even the thought of having children caused me great anxiety. As we deplaned, I wanted to approach the mother of the still screaming toddler and tell her to be vigilant, to never look away, not even for a second.

This was a work weekend for Derek. My husband was an architect, skilled specifically in hip new designs for the hospitality industry. Restaurants and hotels were his bread and butter. Quite often his work took him away on weekends. When we first got together, I loved his career. I would accompany him on business trips to stunningly beautiful destinations. Thailand, Greece, Maui.

Places that were craving a fresh look. Places that were rebranding. Derek loves his job, most likely more than he loves me and that's fine. Derek is a terrific life partner and a true friend, but he is not the love of my life. Henry is. Many facts in life are simply indisputable and this was one of them. Perhaps that's one of the reasons why we never reproduced. I could never love Derek's children completely. I couldn't even love myself completely. Not after what happened.

***

The untouched snow-covered streets of Bar Harbor were the perfect semblance of purity. Pristine and lovely, the scenery commanded the attention of all onlookers. This Christmas morning, I was the only person in sight. Undoubtedly everyone else was occupied by traditions. Christmas sticky buns, coffee sprinkled with a dash of cinnamon, the rustle of wrapping paper, and the sights and sounds of happy little faces. I didn't engage in such traditions, but I thought, this moment right here, *this* could become a Christmas tradition of my own. The serenity of this moment had me slowing down to park on the outskirts of Main Street. I didn't want to disrupt this sleepy little town on Christmas morning. I parked in the first spot I came to, grabbed my backpack, and stepped out into the crisp sea air.

I walked down the center of Main Street toward the pier. The only noise was the crunching of my Bean boots in the snow. That and my breathing, which I found to be strangely soothing as I trudged along. I could see my breath as I walked. It was barely dawn, the sky a flat gray color over the choppy ocean waters. As I started down the hill, I turned to look behind me and saw only my footprints following me. I smiled. It's a rare moment to walk these streets alone. As I approached the park bench, I noticed a car in the parking lot. This lot was not for overnight parking. Did they issue parking tickets on Christmas? I hoped not, but I wouldn't be surprised either.

I wiped the fresh snow off the park bench with my gloved hands and sat down. The cold seat reminded me of the blanket in my bag. I dug it out, stood up, and wrapped it around my body before settling back down on the bench. I looked at the car and noticed no tracks in the snow. This car must have been here early, or really late, to have missed the snow squall. Just then a man stepped out of the car, and I realized it was Henry.

"Hey," I waved to him as he approached. I started to spread my blanket out on the bench, but he tucked it securely back around my legs and sat down on the cold surface.

"Did you stay here all night?" I asked.

"Merry Christmas," he said, swiftly dodging my invasive question.

"Merry Christmas!" I blushed unexpectedly.

"So..." Henry salivated beside me, unable to wait one more second for my response. "What are your thoughts?"

"It's horrifying," I shuddered. "I still haven't digested it all, honestly. I think the more important question is, what are *your* thoughts? Do you have a plan? What do you need me to do?"

"Can we go somewhere and talk?" He looked around his shoulders as if he thought we were being watched.

"Just tell me the short version. I need a hint, at least, of what I'm getting myself into." I shrugged.

"Do you trust me?" he asked.

"No," I snickered at him.

"What? Yes, you do, you let me in your home," he argued.

"I don't know you well enough to trust you yet," I rationalized. "I don't trust you; I just clearly don't value my safety very much."

"Fair enough," he replied.

"And that's not my home," I interjected snippily, "That's my house. I haven't found my home yet."

We sat in silence for a moment. I stewed over why his home comment bothered me so much. After a few minutes, he continued.

"I want you to help me find my daughter. It's my belief, after a year of research, that she is close by. She, and the rest of the girls. There's too many of them to parade all over the place and the disappearances are too close together."

"Makes sense," I nodded even though I wasn't convinced. I remembered the dates being spread out over the last few years.

"There are places here, deep in the woods. Places people pretend to not know about. Places perfect for hiding. I doubt our trusty law enforcement officials dug that deep."

I shivered, not because I was cold.

"It's chilly this morning," Henry rubbed my shoulders as if to generate heat. "Can we go back to your place and keep talking?"

"Sure," I smiled.

An hour later I was cooking us omelets. Living alone, I learned early to become a good cook. I loved watching cooking shows and always tried to duplicate my favorite recipes. Most turned out delicious, others not so much. I struggled to cook fish, which is ironic because I live on the beautiful coast of Maine.

"Did Santa bring you anything for Christmas?" Henry joked over his coffee. We were sitting at the kitchen island eating breakfast.

"Just you," I winked at him.

I'd come to notice the more time we spent together, the easier it felt to let my guard down. It'd be years before I'd realize I use sex as a defense mechanism. It was far easier to sleep with someone than to talk to them. Henry was my needle in a haystack. He forced conversation. Maybe it was because he was uncomfortable with my age, or maybe it was because he was so focused on finding his daughter, either way, he commanded my attention in a professional manner. I was enthralled by him, so happy to have a friend.

"Seriously," he teased me. "No presents? Not even from your parents?"

"Richard and Diane?" My laughter turned into a scoffing chuckle.

"I'm sorry," Henry apologized. "I shouldn't pry."

"No, it's fine," I took another bite of my omelet. Bacon, jalapeno, and cheddar was my go-to concoction nowadays. The flavors melted together into savory goodness every time. I wiped my mouth with my napkin before continuing. "I'm sure there's a gift card in the mail."

We sipped our coffees, letting a welcomed silence settle over us.

"I'm not a holiday person, anyway," I sighed.

"Holidays are for families," Henry said softly. He stared into his coffee like perhaps he could see Suzie there, a reflection of a memory maybe.

"Explain your plan to me," I interrupted the quiet.

"I spent the entire last year searching. I've combed every inch of this island. Every lost cave and abandoned cabin. I've left no stone unturned. But then I got to thinking, if I were holding twenty girls hostage, I'd need assistance. Four or five men anyway, to keep the peace and retrieve supplies. I'd need a big house." Henry had stood up and was pacing the kitchen. He tapped his temple like he'd had a revelation. "This place is littered with affluent homes. Hell, mansions make up most of the side streets. Large home after large home after large home. These girls are hiding in plain sight. They are right here, right under our noses!"

I watched Henry become more and more agitated as he talked. A sickening sadness settled deep into my bones. I knew there was no way these missing girls were all together. The kidnappings had been taking place for years. These girls would be aging, losing value to potential investors. No, these girls were not holed up in a vacation home on Cottage Street. I knew the likelihood was strong that they were distributed shortly after abduction. Someone was getting rich on these innocent lives, stealing and selling them like sports cars. Most of these girls were likely dead by now. I recognized that reality. Henry did not. He seemed set in stone with his theory. As I watched him pace, I wondered what kind of man I was dealing with. Maybe it was because he hadn't slept, maybe he was extremely caffeinated, probably both, but I watched as he spiraled like a toy top, pacing and spinning and barely pausing to breathe. I wasn't sure if I should feel sorry for him or scared for myself. It was heartbreaking, watching him. Finally, I couldn't watch any longer. I walked over and stood in front of him as he leaned against the refrigerator.

"I will help you any way I can," I vowed. I placed both my hands on his pounding chest. I could feel his heart racing through his shirt. "We'll find Suzie." I looked into his eyes as I spoke.

He pulled me close to him, clinging to my frame for dear life. I found comfort in his embrace. I felt his heartbeat slow as his body melted into mine.

Neither one of us spoke as I directed us through the foyer and into the living room. We sat down on the couch and I snuggled into his side. It was then that I realized I hadn't slept either. It was also then that I realized the power of touch. My essence seemed to thrive just being near him. A peacefulness blanketed the both of us and we slept.

Four

When we awoke a few hours later, the snow was really coming down outside. Here in Downeast Maine, the weather can be unpredictable at best and when winter settles in, all bets are off. There's a common saying in Maine: 'If you don't like the weather, wait five minutes'. Again, if I'd paid attention during meteorology, I might know why. Quite often there was no snow at all on Christmas. I'd seen people mow their lawns on Christmas Day. I much prefer clean white snow to the earthy undertones of Winter. I'd often thought people should hibernate too, like bears, or trees even, shaking off their dead leaves only to rest and then grow new ones. Humans don't rest. Not like trees and bears.

Henry and I both wore the same clothes as the previous day, but neither of us seemed to care. We ordered more Chinese food, thankful for an open restaurant on Christmas. Henry didn't talk much. I wondered if he was emotionally drained. I knew if I wanted answers, I'd have to ask questions. His mind seemed to be stalled like he was lost in a trance. I wished I knew what he was thinking about but part of me was relieved I did not.

"Do you have any pictures of when you were little?" he asked curtly. His question took me by surprise.

"I don't," I shook my head. "Just the family photo in the dining room."

"No pictures?" his voice sounded dismal.

"Nope. Never anyone around to take pictures."

"That's quite sad," he whispered.

"It's fine," I lied.

"What is it your parents do for work?" he inquired.

"I'm not exactly sure," I replied. Wanting to change the subject, I interjected my next question hastily and without thinking. "How long were you and your wife married?" When he didn't respond, I immediately apologized. "I'm sorry, we don't have to talk about her."

"Catherine," he said, his voice low.

"We can talk about something else. I just..." I struggled for the right words. "I want you to know I want to help."

"Thank you," he sighed heavily then stood up abruptly. "I need to go home. Thank you for having me here."

With that, he left.

I laid down on the couch and stared up out the window at the blustering snow globe around me. This house had so many windows, so much light streamed in when it was daytime, but also so much darkness when the light vanished. I pulled a warm fuzzy blanket up around my shoulders. I couldn't get Henry out of my mind. At this point in our association, I had noticed several red flags. I say association because I couldn't figure him out. I couldn't say friendship. We weren't friends. He was still pretty much a stranger, becoming more and more strange by the minute, it seemed. Relationship wasn't the correct word either. Acquaintance, maybe? Either way, there were things that didn't settle right with me. Things that made me more and more curious.

Henry was a mystery. His edginess had me questioning my judgment. His abruptness in leaving made me uncomfortable. The way he paced around my kitchen when he told me his theory behind the kidnappings had made me wonder about my own safety for a second, just a millisecond really. I'd pushed my apprehensions away immediately. His asking me for pictures had sent a chill up my spine that I couldn't ignore. I rationalized it though, by telling myself it was Christmas and he missed his daughter. He couldn't be a bad guy. He'd had ample time to attack me but he hadn't. He could have easily made sexual advances but he hadn't. I had!

As I watched the snow descend like lace curtains falling to the ground, I thought about the missing girls. For a brief moment, I thought I should take the file to the police. I should corroborate his story. They could tell me in seconds if this information was accurate or made up. What kind of person would concoct such a story? Certainly, this scheme was too complex to be fiction. My responsible, almost adult side told me I should get off the couch right this second and drive to the police station to verify Henry's story. My still adolescent, lonely, compassionate side told me not to say a word, to enjoy Henry's company, to believe him, and to help him. I had no idea how I was supposed to help but I knew Henry needed me. And I needed him. I'd been happier in the last twenty-four hours than I had been in my whole life. Yes, I needed Henry, maybe more than he needed me. I couldn't take the chance of the authorities telling me Henry was a fraud, a delusional inmate who escaped from the Maine State Prison in Warren, or a psychotic person who should be under lock and key. Everyone had a little bit of delusional craziness in them, right? Beyond that, what if he was telling the truth and I refused to help him? It was too late for that now. I was in this for the long haul. I would help him reunite with Suzie. Lord knows I needed some purpose in my life. To be almost eighteen and feel so empty, so forgotten, so neglected, was not something I would wish on anyone.

As dusk settled in, I realized I'd survived another Christmas. It was always such a lonely time of year for people without families, for people who aren't loved. I decided to shower and sleep, both things I desperately needed.

***

Two weeks passed and I didn't hear anything from Henry. Two weeks of heart-wrenching setbacks for me. Henry had boosted my ego, and my confidence, so much. He'd spiced up my otherwise extremely dull life and his absence felt like a crippling blow to my spirit. I knew it was probably for the best. Clearly, I was too attached, too broken, like a ragged screen door that couldn't open, hanging crookedly on busted rusty hinges.

I had originally thought Henry was broken; I knew now it was me. I craved attention. It was unhealthy. Unhealthy to the point where I'd gone to the same spot where Henry and I met, every day. The people working on the other side of the window of the classic country store probably wished I'd come inside and purchase something. I didn't. I aimlessly gazed in the window at their display of Maine comfort items. Cast iron skillets ranging in different sizes, blueberry recipe books, homemade mittens, and jars of Maine-made maple syrup were nestled inside handmade wooden crates and surrounded by fake snow. Someone had taken great time and consideration to strategically place white string lights throughout the display.

When the clerk came outside one day and asked if she could help me find something, I finally decided to move on, get a grip on myself, and grow up. My birthday had come and gone. Henry was, well…I'm not sure what Henry was, but he wasn't interested in me. That part was clear. Maybe he'd been a figment of my imagination, concocted out of desperation and loneliness. I couldn't find the folder. He must have taken it when he left. No one else had been in my house and my backpack was empty. The only evidence of Henry's existence had been a fridge full of Chinese. I was starting to question my sanity.

As I turned away from the window I'd been staring into for two weeks, I bumped directly into another body. Instinctively I thought it was Henry. I closed my eyes on impact as our bodies collided and when I reopened them I realized it wasn't Henry at all. It was a woman, a lady my age, or so it appeared at first glance. As we steadied ourselves, I was free to notice my accidental assailant. My breath caught in my throat as I stood there looking into Molly's eyes.

"Molly?" I barely whispered her name.

She looked at me with a wild, scared expression.

"It's me, Ryan, from school." I reached out to touch her arm, to steady her reassuringly. She winced at my touch, her eyes wide. "Molly..." I started to speak and as I did, she backed up, slowly at first, and then her feet were tangled together as she tripped and fell to the sidewalk. I looked at her hunched on the ground, scared, almost in tears. Her dress was torn, her eyes wild with an emotion I'd never seen: terror.

"Molly, I know," I said urgently. "I know what's going on. Come with me. I'll help you!"

She didn't speak. She crawled away from the spot where she'd fallen on her hands and knees, scurrying away from me. I walked toward her slowly and tried to help her stand up. She turned around and looked up at me like a rabid animal.

"Don't!" she hissed.

"Molly, it's me! Ryan! We had homeroom together. Please, let me help you! I know you've been kidnapped. I know what's going on. Let me help you! Come home with me."

"Don't," she hissed again. "You'll only make it worse!" With that, she got to her feet and ran away.

That was the first moment I hated Henry. I had no idea where he was or what he was up to. I had no way to get a hold of him, no way to report in. I wanted to yell and scream. I'd just seen Molly! Molly, who was on the list of missing girls. I needed to tell him, but I couldn't do a damn thing. Frustration streamed down my face.

"Dear, are you alright?" an elderly lady's voice sounded from beside me. I turned to see a familiar face, the clerk from the store where I'd bought my lamp on Christmas Eve. I wiped my eyes, smudging them more than drying them. I looked at her, wishing she could help me somehow.

"I hope you're loving the Christmas lamp," she said as she reached out. I let her pat my arm reassuringly.

"I am," I cried.

"Oh dear," she clucked at me.

I attempted a smile and slowly started walking away. I stopped when I felt her tug on my jacket.

"Honey," she whispered. "I know it's none of my business and an old lady ought to keep her nose out of where it doesn't belong, but I just have to say, be careful with that man."

"What man?" I tried to keep the alarm out of my voice.

"The man you were with when you bought the lamp." She patted my arm again and walked away.

I stood there frozen as I watched her get into her car and drive away. Be careful with that man? Really? Say something so cryptic and walk away? My doubt of Henry's reliability had vanished the moment I saw Molly. I knew he wasn't lying. Now the clerk's futile attempt to warn me had me questioning everything all over again. Who exactly was Henry?

Later that evening as I lay in bed scanning through TV channels, I realized I was in too deep to get out. I paused instinctively on a local news channel, a shiver shooting up my spine as I recognized the car being towed from the water. I wasn't sure, but I thought I could see a slumped-over driver draped around the steering wheel. I couldn't look away from the car. It looked an awful lot like the vehicle I'd seen the clerk get into earlier today.

The news anchorman was calling it an accident but from somewhere deep in my gut I knew it was not. It was Henry. My body quivered. I turned the television off and lay quietly in the dark thinking about my options. Doing nothing was not an option, not after seeing Molly today. I could go to the cops and report everything, but would they believe me? I'd sound like a lunatic with no proof. I could cut ties with Henry altogether, although it seemed he'd already beaten me to it. I silently considered each option, forgetting the most obvious one. Play along. I could be smart. I knew, or at least I thought I knew what was going on. From the clerk's dire warning, in addition to Henry's edginess and disappearing act, not to forget how he creepily asked for my childhood pictures, I was fairly certain Henry was the one we should be looking out for. Maybe he was delusional, making up this entire scheme. Maybe he took the girls. Either way, I knew he was a wild card. I could play along, knowing this information and keeping it tucked away, and maybe I could get closer to some answers.

Three days later I attended the funeral service for Rose, the elderly clerk who most likely died protecting me. The church was full, most likely a testament to Rose's life. She was a godly woman, a true friend to everyone she met. She would be sorely missed in the community. I stood in the rear of the church, not wanting human interaction. As soon as the eulogy finished, I quietly snuck out the heavy church doors. As I hurried down the stone steps something to the right of the church yard caught my eye. Someone had tripped and fallen, someone with a Carhartt jacket, a man. I hurried to help him up but by the time I got there, he had scurried to his feet already. I grabbed his jacket as he started away from me and I caught a big enough glimpse of his face to tell it was Henry.

"Henry!" I yelled at him, astonished that he'd just walk away from me. "Maybe you are a psycho!"

He stopped at the word and slowly turned around to face me. He quickly closed the gap between us, his index finger wagging in my face.

"Who told you that? Did that bitch tell you that?" He pointed to the church.

"No! Henry..." I shook my head.

"Is that what she was saying to you the other day?" he seethed.

"Is that why you killed her?" I seethed back.

He instantly deflated, taking two steps backward.

"I didn't, I don't... How do you...?" He muttered.

"Henry, listen to me, I don't care!" I took his hands in mine. "I saw Molly! I believe you! Please, let me help!" I begged.

He didn't speak, but he gripped my hand and led me down Kennebec Street and into what I assumed was his home. So close to civilization. So close to the church and the park. To children. So inconspicuously placed beside the fire and police stations. I smiled up at him as he led me up the front steps. He didn't look like a killer and if he were one, his hiding in broad daylight seemed to be working well for him.

He closed the door behind me and motioned for me to lead the way down the small narrow hallway. I stepped into the kitchen and my breath caught in my throat when I saw her. There she was, Molly, making sandwiches at the L-shaped bar. She looked up at me when I gasped and when she saw Henry behind me, she quickly averted her eyes back to the ham and cheese.

To this day, I'm not a sandwich girl. No ham and cheese, or turkey and Swiss, or roast beef. I don't like soggy bread. If I do eat a sandwich it has to be grilled. Golden, crispy, buttery deliciousness was comfort food. Even now, Derek knows I can be won over any day with a good grilled cheese and bacon sandwich. At this moment though, I was not concerned with lunch.

There were several milestones in my relationship with Henry where I knew I'd gone too far, yet each time I ignored reality, stepping closer, sinking deeper, falling harder. This was one of those moments.

"What's going on?" I turned to Henry as I spoke. "What is she doing here?" When he didn't answer me, I turned to Molly. "What are you doing here?" I asked her, confused.

"I took her," Henry cut in, answering so Molly wouldn't.

"What do you mean, you took her?" I swallowed hard, not wanting to know the answer.

"Just like I'm taking you," he looked down at the linoleum floor as he spoke. "I watched her, then I took her. It's not hard."

My heart beat loudly in my ears, and my mouth suddenly dry. I stood in front of him, anxious to be taken.

"Well," I rationalized. "If I'm here now, you can let her go."

"You mean, you'll stay? Willingly?" his eyes were slits looking at me, his expression forlorn and doubtful.

"Yes," I bit my bottom lip. "I'll stay willingly, but you have to let her go."

He stared at me before he started pacing. I watched Molly continue to make sandwiches. Her wrists were red and bruised like she'd been pulling against restraints.

"I can't," he muttered. "Can't, can't, can't."

"Why not?" I asked softly.

"She'll talk. She'll tell on me. She'll press charges. They'll take me and I'll never find Suzie."

"Okay, well, let's ask her. Alright?" I transformed into the mediator I never knew I could be. Henry nodded. "Molly, if Henry lets you leave, are you going to press charges? Clearly, he made a mistake. Right, Henry?"

"Yes," Henry's head bobbed away like a dashboard ornament. "Mistake, yes, it was a mistake. I'm sorry, Molly, I'm sorry. Please don't tell."

As I looked at him, I thought he resembled a frightened fourteen-year-old boy. The kind of boy who was begging the cops not to tell his parents he was shoplifting. This was kidnapping, and Lord knows what else, and Henry was acting like a scared teenager.

"I won't tell," Molly promised.

"What would you tell people?" I asked her. We needed a plan.

"I'll say I can't remember anything." She had looked up from the sandwiches now. Henry kept pacing on the other side of the kitchen. I nodded to Molly, motioning my head in the direction of the door and mouthing the word 'go'. She slowly stepped away from the countertop and backed toward me until I was positioned between them. She looked at me with concern in her eyes.

"It's okay, I'll help him. We're friends," I smiled reassuringly.

I didn't have to tell her twice. She turned and ran down the short hallway and out the front door. I should have told her that her family moved but there was no time for pleasantries. I slowly walked over to where Henry had stopped pacing and was standing beside the small round kitchen table.

"She didn't want to stay here," he acknowledged defeatedly.

"No," I agreed. "But I do. I'll stay."

He looked at me as if seeing me for the first time. I stepped closer to him and wrapped my shaking arms around his steady calm body. He brushed at my hair with his fingers, twirling the ends of my dark curls, before returning my embrace, locking his arms around my body in an enchanting surrender. We held each other and I could feel relief flood through his core. Moments later he sat at the table while I plated the sandwiches Molly had made. I poured us each a glass of milk and we ate lunch in silence. Henry appeared slightly dazed, and I was contemplating what the fuck kind of situation I'd gotten myself into.

Five

Age is one of the biggest aspects of life that is of no real relevance. I didn't see age. Perhaps it was because I'd lived such a life of solitude. Perhaps it was because I never had a father. Perhaps it was because I enjoyed going against the grain. Either way, I refused to see the danger in Henry even though I *knew* it was there. He had lived two lives to my one. He was double my age, yet I felt drawn to him in an unexplainable way.

Henry showed me the house after we finished our lunch, assuring me there were no more girls hidden in the basement or attic. His house was older, weathered, and less attractive than the newer models, but it somehow felt homey regardless.

"I watched her for weeks," he admitted later that night as we lay in bed.

He'd given me a pair of his wife's pajamas. They were light blue, flannel, and dotted with snowflakes. Perfect for winter. Catherine and I were just about the same size. Henry lay clothed on top of the blankets while I snuggled warmly beneath them. He had been nothing but polite and welcoming since I switched places with Molly.

"I thought she was helping them," he continued. "She would grocery shop alone a few times a week. Alone. By herself. Who grocery shops that often? And she always bought feminine products like there was going to be a shortage."

Henry didn't know that Molly's mother had passed away the year before or that Molly was the oldest of four teenage daughters. Of course they used a lot of feminine products.

"I bumped into her outside the grocery store one day, quite similar to how I bumped into you. I befriended her."

"She didn't seem like she was your friend," I barely whispered.

"Yeah," he said, his voice trailing off to a place I couldn't follow. He seemed fragile, like china that had just been glued back together.

"Are you lying to me, Henry?" I blurted out before I could filter my thoughts.

"Excuse me?" He sat up.

"Are you lying?" I repeated the insulting question.

"About what?" He seemed genuinely confused.

"About anything." My voice sounded bolder than I felt. "I'm happy to stay here with you, Henry. I'm happy to help in any way I can. But I won't be another Molly. I will not be trapped here."

"I don't want to trap you," his face looked worn even now in the shadowy darkness of his bedroom.

"Why didn't you let her go when you realized you'd made a mistake?" I asked the question I didn't want to know the answer to.

"I didn't want to be alone," he said, his voice monotone and cold. Desperation will make people do unthinkable things.

"I have to be able to trust you, Henry, if I'm going to stay here. We have to trust each other." My voice was foreign to me like I'd somehow evolved into a therapist.

"We'll start training tomorrow," he replied.

A few moments later he was snoring next to me, and I was left wondering what he meant by training. I had no idea what I was getting myself into, but I wasn't scared in the least bit. I felt like the grown-up, like the one in charge. Henry didn't scare me; I felt concerned for him. Maybe he was mentally unstable, slower than the rest of us. I hadn't noticed it at first. His temperament had been sweet, charming even, when we first bumped into each other. Then at the cafe, he'd been edgy. At the park, he'd been a real gentleman. At my house, he'd been very sweet with the Christmas tree before he switched back to being edgy again. He was like flipping a coin, you either got his sweet side or his tense side. For some reason, I saw sweet Henry most of the time. The poor store clerk's last image of this world certainly wasn't of sweet

Henry. I closed my eyes, wondering which Henry I'd wake up to in the morning.

***

How does one learn to decipher the truth from a lie? How does one become a victim of gullibility? You think you can trust your instincts, that you know what your abilities and pitfalls are. You think you're able to live a life without doubts until you can't. Once you start questioning yourself is it game over or is it the gunshot at the starting line ringing in your ears, signaling that the race has finally begun? Everything up until now has only been practice.

When we first started training, we used foam darts and Nerf guns. Henry had me sit on the couch and told me to cover one eye with my hand and stare straight ahead, not resting my eyesight on a specific part of his body, but rather watching all of him. Not focusing. He would then aim the gun at me, which I was not to look at. I would wait and watch for the signal, and I never knew what it was going to be. A quick finger flip, a leg spasm, a wink, whichever side of his body moved, that was the way I should move. Just a little, barely moving, pretending I was being held hostage from behind, a knife at my throat perhaps.

I learned to watch Henry's profile, to depict his next move. At first, the Nerf darts shot my neck, my head, my ears. They bounced off my flesh painlessly. It's hard to mirror someone's directions. Is their left my left? You have to shut your mind off, giving complete control only to your eyes. You have to surrender the rest of you. Slowly I learned to follow Henry's fingers, his eyes, and the twitch of his mouth. Slowly the darts missed me altogether and thumped into the sofa. Not so slowly, my temperature started to rise. Henry made me sweaty. He made my heart pound, and my legs quiver. Remaining still became the hardest part.

"Henry, what do you want me to do? How am I going to help?" I asked a few days into my training.

"I want you to go door to door and search people's houses," he responded while he loaded the Nerf gun.

"Door to door here?" I chuckled, a bit surprised. I shouldn't have been. I knew his theory was that the girls were being held close by. It was the same theory that made him zero in on Molly. I tried not to think about Molly. I didn't want to imagine what he might have done to her. I wanted him to remain as untainted as possible. We also never spoke of Rose. Maybe her death had been an accident. Maybe he had nothing to do with it at all. If I didn't know, both mine and Henry's innocence could remain intact.

"Yes, door to door, specifically the big homes," he explained.

"The big homes?" I repeated.

"Yes."

"May I ask why?" I tried not to sound irritated.

"Why what?" he was confused.

"Why the big homes? I mean, Henry, come on. Do you think they are each in a cozy room, binging Netflix and having tea parties?" I asked curtly, my attempts to disguise my frustration had failed. He didn't respond. He just looked at me aimlessly.

"Henry," I continued softly. "Henry, these girls aren't together."

He didn't speak. He simply lifted the Nerf gun and we continued.

I got so I craved our training. I needed it. It soothed me. Sometimes I could even feel my attacker behind me. I could feel his heartbeat against my back. I could feel his breath against my hair and when Henry shot the gun, I could feel my assailant's blood splatter against my neck. It made me wet, everywhere.

After nearly a year of research, I knew Henry wouldn't throw in the towel so easily. He had his heels dug in. Any attempts I made at redirecting his logic were acutely ignored. Despite that, Henry and I grew closer. He slept under the covers with me at night. We even started going out together. We'd go out to dinner and then drive Acadia's Park Loop Road, watching the beautiful sunset, usually in silence. Henry was impossible to figure out. I always wondered what he was thinking about, but I never dared to ask. Not at first.

No one else ever warned me about Henry, either. Rose was the only one and the more time I spent with Henry, the more I questioned her validity. Maybe she had confused Henry with someone else. He was nothing short of a gentleman with me. The more time we spent together the less edgy he became. It was like he just needed someone to trust him, and he needed to trust someone else. We both needed each other, at least that's what I thought.

"Can I tell you my theory?" I broached the subject one night after dinner.

"Yes," he said smiling. He reached across the table and touched my hand affectionately. His touch calmed my nervous shake. I didn't want to upset him. "I'm sorry I've been so unapproachable," he added. "I just want to find them."

I squeezed his hand in mine and continued holding it while I spoke.

"I think you can't worry about all the other girls. I think you need to focus on Suzie. She needs you.

I'm sure the other girls have people looking for them. I don't think you can save them all." I felt his hand start to pull away and I squeezed it tighter, holding it in place with mine. "It's commendable of you to want to save them all, Henry, of course. I'm sure everyone wants to save them all but that's not practical. Henry, those girls were probably sold off to the highest bidder as soon as they were taken. It's my theory though, that Suzie was not. Her kidnapping was not intentional. The guy only wanted the car. He didn't even want Catherine. By the time he realized Suzie was in the back seat, it was too late to change course. He'd just killed her mother in front of her. Suzie was a liability, not an asset. I think whoever is in charge of the whole operation kept her."

"Kept her." He repeated my words more as a statement than a question.

"Yes. For reasons we may never know. Maybe they grew a conscience with a younger-than-usual steal. Maybe they thought of her as a second chance. I don't know."

"A second chance?" He twirled his thumb around mine slowly.

"I've thought about this a lot. A lot, a lot." I shook my head as if to clear it. "I can't imagine people in charge of sex trade industries are very happy. Loaded, yes, very rich. But happy? Fulfilled? Family-focused? No. Take my parents, for instance. Never home, wealthy, sophisticated. They'd one hundred percent fit the profile."

"You think your parents have Suzie?" He sat back in his seat, looking almost shocked at my proposition.

"I don't know," I insisted. "I'm just saying it's a believable theory. I mean, I'm over ten years older than Suzie. My existence is an afterthought. I'm almost forgotten." Henry sat forward and took my hand again as I continued. "I wasn't planned or wanted. I'm a mistake. Now fast forward ten years, a little girl mistakenly lands in their laps. I bet they'd consider that a do-over. A chance to redeem themselves for practically throwing away their first child. Maybe this is bullshit. I don't know. But maybe it's not."

"So, we need to find your parents," Henry concluded.

"Well, that's what I mean. How many people have no idea where their parents live? Isn't that odd?"

"That is odd," he agreed.

"Maybe I could hire an investigator or private detective. Someone to trace paper trails, receipts, bank transfers," I stared out the window as I spoke now.

"Have you talked to them lately?" he asked.

"No, but I need to. I need to give them my decision about the house." I stood up and started clearing the table.

"If you're going to stay there or move?" Henry helped me clean.

"Yes," I said softly.

"What are you going to say?" he asked cautiously, as if he were afraid of my answer.

"Well," I said as I put our leftover lasagna in the fridge. "I live here with you now, so I guess it's up to you."

"Up to me?" He stopped loading the dishwasher and looked at me. "How is it up to me?"

"Well, if you want me to keep living here, with you, I'll tell them I don't want the house. I'll be with you."

"You...you'd do that?" He looked at me in awe.

Looking back, I realize I attached myself to Henry quite quickly. Again, maybe it was the danger aspect, but I think it was more of a companionship addiction. I didn't want to live in my big house void of love, void of family, void of any memories that mattered. I didn't tell Henry that my parents would put more money than the house's value in my bank account if I moved out. Money didn't seem to be an issue for Henry. I often wondered what he did for work before his life became consumed with vengeance.

I stepped closer to him, leaned down, closed the open dishwasher, and took yet another step toward him so we were face to face.

"I love you, Henry," I said. "And I'm sorry you've been dealt this hand in life. If you want me to, I will live here with you. I will be with you in whatever capacity you'd like. You just have to tell me what you want." My eyes blazed into his as I waited for his reply.

"Stay here with me," he whispered, tipping my chin up towards him. He pressed his lips to mine and I felt myself unravel in his arms. I clung to him and he to me, both of us in desperate need of each other for survival. Neither of us spoke as he took me to his bedroom and laid me down. He touched me, his fingers like fire against my skin, burning my clothes away, and his, so we were bare against each other. His body pressed into mine, firm and hard, desire flowing freely between us like sand in an hourglass. Were we doomed from the start? Our time together destined to run out? It doesn't matter either way; I know I wouldn't have changed a thing.

The next day we carried on as if we had been together for years. There was no more discussion about relationships or labels. We just lived.

"When you tell your parents you don't want the house, what will they say? How does that go?" Henry asked me over breakfast the next morning.

"I think I just have to go sign some documents," I said between bites of toast.

"How about this? We could follow them after you sign the papers. Maybe they will lead us to Suzie." Hope sparkled in Henry's eyes as he spoke.

"They most likely won't go in person," I sighed.

"Oh. Well, maybe their address will be on the paperwork."

"For sure," I agreed. "And I'm close with their attorney. I can get their address. Honestly, I just haven't needed it over the years. They've always had a PO box here in town and if I ever needed anything I would text them or tell their assistant."

"If you do this, does this mean you're cutting ties with them for me?" he inquired.

"I'm cutting ties with them for me," I assured him. "This is nothing more than a business transaction."

"It's way more than that," he said. "Way more."

With Henry, I always felt like I was home. No matter what was going on, no matter what we were doing, I always felt secure. Henry made me feel good. We continued my Nerf gun training even though I knew if my theory was correct the gun would be real, not Nerf, and it would be pointed at Richard and Diane. I didn't care. I felt loyal to Henry. I felt loved. And that was something I'd never felt before. It was an emotion I chose not to question, even though I knew none of it made any logical sense. Logic was often boring; this I knew as clearly as the sky is blue and water is wet. I'd lived my entire life thus far against the grain and even though it was lonely at times, it was something I was proud of. I wasn't a robot conforming to the norms of society and although my loneliness hadn't been my choice, I had learned to find solace in the stillness. Hadn't I? Or was the fact that I latched onto Henry so unapologetically a sign that perhaps I was the emotionally disturbed one? I convinced myself I was helping him, hopefully even healing him, as I sat still and let Nerf darts skim my face. It became our foreplay. But was he the one healing me? Watching over me? Studying me? We fed off each other, our lives intertwined in ways I couldn't even begin to comprehend.

Over the next few months, I became more and more convinced my parents were the villains. I'd stealthily seen their residential address and it had been a fake one. What kind of people use a fake address on a legal document? Maybe it happened more than I realized, but I thought it seemed suspicious. What reason could they possibly have for lying?

I had thirty days to vacate the premises, as I'd told them I wasn't concerned about finding housing. I ransacked the house before I left. My family home held no semblance of family. As I packed and took what I wanted, I scanned each crevice and corner for anything that might give me a clue as to their real identities and whereabouts. When I'd searched their names online there was nothing more than the usual boring information. I'd even hired a detective, but he had no leads. I'd begun to wonder if he worked for them.

Henry and I grew closer, and I saw my doctor about contraception. When I went to pay the bill, I was told it was already taken care of. I should have been happy to still be on their insurance, but instead, I was furious. I told the receptionist I was eighteen now and wanted them off my account. She smiled at me like it was the next natural step and handed me pamphlets for free healthcare and sliding scale policies. I left feeling good. I felt empowered like I was headed in the right direction. I felt like I had a clean slate like I could be anyone I wanted to be. I didn't have to be attached to them anymore. Lord knows they weren't attached to me. I felt like even though I was taking baby steps, at least I was walking.

Six

As fall crept upon us, I decided one afternoon that I needed to slow down and breathe a bit. I stopped my car on the back side of the park and sat on a bench to do nothing more than watch the leaves change. It felt like fall came earlier and earlier every year. The summer months were so scarce, squeezed together by the more demanding seasons, like bookends too full, so full that the books in the middle pushed out in protest.

I sat there mindlessly counting the leaves that fell, the early leaves that just couldn't hold on any longer. I watched a girl with orange hair as she tried to catch each falling leaf. She played fearlessly as the leaves fell aimlessly from the trees above. As I watched her I thought of how great my life was.

Yes, Henry and I were engaged with our underlying mission, but we had bonded. I loved him. He had so effortlessly become my world. There was no explanation other than fate.

As I watched the little girl, lost in my own thoughts, a woman who had been parked in a car across the street hollered out to her. "Suzie, come on! It's time to go."

My head snapped in her direction as I watched the girl wait and look for traffic before crossing the street and getting in the backseat of the charcoal 4Runner. I jumped up and ran as fast as my legs would carry me but by the time I reached the street, the car had driven away.

"Fuck!" I screamed. People stopped to stare at my outburst. I ran back to my car and sped away in search of the boxy SUV. I followed the winding road, hoping to catch sight of the 4Runner. The fall tourist season was underway and that meant old folks driving well under the speed limit to peak at the foliage. No doubt it was a beautiful backdrop to the sparkling ocean water, but the only color I wanted to see right now was dark gray.

As I neared closer to the ferry lot, something in my gut told me to turn into the Park n' Ride. I drove slowly down the rows of vehicles, desperately searching for the Toyota. I was about to give up, throw in the towel, and retreat when I noticed curly carrot-colored hair bouncing along, hurrying to keep up with a woman dressed in a fashionable pantsuit. It was her. It was Suzie. I'd recognize her anywhere. I hadn't been paying attention at the park. Every ounce of my being wanted to chase after them, but then what? I didn't recognize the woman she was with. I didn't know how to proceed. I sat back in my seat and worked to control my breathing. I didn't want to blow this for Henry. No, I wouldn't do that. This was a good thing, a great thing! Now at least we had a direction to look in. Maybe they were just taking the ferry to Nova Scotia for a day trip. They didn't have any luggage. Did they live in Canada? I hadn't thought of that. Canada was a stone's throw away, a quick ferry ride up the Atlantic.

I parked my car and watched the entrance until the CAT floated out to sea then I went inside and quickly scanned the ferry station. They were gone. As I walked back to my car, I thought about what I would tell Henry. I hoped he wasn't mad because I let them get away. By the time I arrived home, I'd worked myself into quite a frenzy. I didn't want to tell him, but I had to. I rushed up the front steps, anxious to see him, but when I got inside he was asleep on the couch. He looked so peaceful sleeping. I went to our bedroom and packed us each a couple changes of clothes. I grabbed our passports, thankful he had his. I walked down the hall to Suzie's room and grabbed her blanket and favorite stuffie. Then I stood in front of the couch and let the bag land on the floor with a thud. Henry didn't stir. I knelt to wake him.

"Henry," I shook his shoulder as I spoke. "Henry, wake up. Henry, we have to go."

He woke up yawning and looked at me sleepily.

"Henry, come on. Let's go. I saw Suzie!"

"What?" He swung his legs over the side of the couch and stood up in seconds.

"Come on, I'll explain in the car. They took the ferry to Canada."

Henry ran to the hall closet and grabbed his black duffle bag. I'd seen him handle the bag several times. Oftentimes he would get it out to clean his guns and check his supplies. Zip ties, Duct tape, flashlights, hoodies, you know, all the essentials.

"Did you get the passports?" he asked as we jumped in the car.

"I did."

"Okay now tell me what happened," he turned to me from the passenger seat.

"I was sitting at the park when a little redheaded girl got into a gray 4Runner. The driver called her Suzie." I explained.

"How tall was she?" I found the question to be awkward but I respected his need for details.

"I was on the other side of the park. I don't know, four feet maybe." I shrugged.

"Four feet?" He raised one eyebrow at me.

"Kid-sized, Henry! Now focus!" I reprimanded him sharply, surprising even myself. "I followed the car to the ferry depot. I watched them walk inside. I know it was her!"

"Oh my God!" he whispered excitedly.

"We've never even talked about Canada," I went on. "It makes sense. It makes perfect sense."

"Who was she with?" he asked.

A woman in a pantsuit. Not my mother. I doubt they'd come here, especially during daylight hours. Maybe she was an assistant? She looked like an assistant.

"How did Suzie look?" His voice cracked at the question.

"Good, I think," I nodded. "I mean she didn't appear to be scared or hurt. She wasn't being forced to walk or anything like that.'

"You really saw her?" His voice sounded fragile. Exquisite, like a marble rolling across a sea of smokey glass.

"She had almost orange hair. She answered to Suzie. It was her, Henry," I grabbed his hand and squeezed it as I drove. "I'm sorry I let her slip away. I hope you don't hate me."

"I could never hate you," he said as he pressed my fingers to his lips.

I pulled into the ferry parking lot for the second time that afternoon. We drove around slowly as we searched for the 4Runner. I hadn't seen it earlier, but now I could see it was tucked away in the back corner of the long-term parking section. We stopped in front of it and got out to investigate but the car was locked and clean—no toys on the floor or evidence of a child's presence. We wrote down the license plate number and I waited while Henry dug through his bag and pulled out a small square black device. I watched as he scooched down to the ground and placed the device up under the car's midsection. He got back in the car with me and we parked in a parking spot closer to the entrance where we could watch people coming and going. The ride to Nova Scotia took three and a half hours. We still had hours until the boat returned.

"What do you want to do?" I asked.

"I say we wait and see if they get back off the ferry." He loaded one gun and handed it to me.

"We haven't practiced this yet," I swallowed hard.

"I know, but I trust you. I need to get my daughter back. I need your help. Please," he begged.

With each moment that passed, I could feel Suzie slipping further and further away. We waited for the ferry to return; neither of us spoke. I knew what he was thinking. I knew I'd let him down. I'd let my mind distract me from our mission. Hours later, we waited in the lobby for the ship's passengers to disembark. When the last set of feet hit American soil, I turned to Henry in anticipation of directions.

"We have no idea where to go if we follow them," he said quietly. "Maybe it's best to wait here and watch the 4Runner."

Relief flooded through me. I was all for a fun adventure, but I knew as well as he did that we'd never find them over there. The deep blue sea covered their tracks. At least here we had their car. We could stay vigilant here and wait for their return.

Henry and I didn't speak the entire ride home and I couldn't sleep at all that night. My mistake weighed on me like an oversized blanket of guilt. It wasn't even a mistake. It was more like absent-mindedness. I'd watched that girl, Suzie, play in the leaves, unaware that it was her for probably close to fifteen minutes. Minutes that were now lost. Minutes that I should have been rescuing her. The only thing was that she didn't appear to need rescuing. She seemed like a normal, happy little girl. If I hadn't heard her name called out, I would have never given her a second thought.

Now, Henry snored in the bed next to me. I was grateful for his noises. He'd been so quiet all night. I couldn't blame him. He *had* to be disappointed in me, mad even. I was. I slowly climbed out of bed, careful not to wake him, and I tiptoed down the hallway to Suzie's room. Henry hadn't touched a thing since her abduction. Her bed was made with a purple patchwork quilt and pale yellow bedsheets. Her floor was a plush dark purple rug. Her twin bed sat in the middle of the room and a small wooden desk was situated under the window. Suzie was a girl who loved Barbies and horses. She had stacks and stacks of Babysitter Club books on her headboard. I rolled back her closet door and found clear Rubbermaid totes of old schoolwork and outgrown clothes. This was a typical girl's room, complete with sparkly unicorn curtains and a full-length mirror on the wall. It was similar to my room growing up, only a quarter of the size.

"What are you doing in here?" Henry's voice startled me.

"Nothing, really," I shrugged. "I just wanted to feel close to her."

Henry took my hand and gently led me out of the room.

"Henry, I'm so sorry," I apologized for the fifteenth time. "I know I let you down. I'm so sorry."

He closed Suzie's bedroom door and turned to me. He didn't say a word as he stepped closer to me, pushing me back forcefully. He put his hand around my neck until his long fingertips hit the wall behind me. All my blood rushed to the surface of my skin. I stayed still, held in place by his strong hand. He pressed his body into mine and I could tell he was aroused. I swallowed sharply, feeling my throat against his hand as I tried to control my breathing. Was I scared or excited? A mixture of both emotions flowed through my veins, each overpowering the other. I tried to bite my lip, but

I couldn't quite close my mouth. The force of his hand around my throat had my reflexes alert and curious as to what he would do next.

"I told you to stop apologizing," he leaned in and whispered in my ear. "Didn't I say that?" His mouth moved to my lips now, softly grazing my cheek first. "I'm not mad," he said reassuringly before he kissed me. I could tell from his mouth touching mine that he was telling the truth. He was not mad. "I'm closer than I've ever been to finding her and it's all because of you."

As he talked and kissed me, I felt myself relax enough to tell that his hand around my neck was not hurting me at all. He was barely touching me. I was the one who was forcing my throat into his palm. It aroused me and I leaned into his lips, bringing my hands up to caress his biceps. Henry was a beautiful, well-sculpted man. I'd been noticing his figure more and more these days, often picturing him in the wee morning hours or when I showered. I couldn't help but fantasize. Now, I let him lead me into the bedroom, where we proved our loyalty to each other over and over until the sun came up.

Henry's age didn't bother me, and my age didn't bother him. We were too busy living our very adult lives together. Suzie was always the priority, other than bedtime when we allowed ourselves the freedom of release and rejuvenation. Henry was my first lover and although I knew I was far from his first, I was grateful for his experience. He was a kind and patient teacher and I was more than happy to be putty in his hands.

Derek has never been a terrific lover. He tries, and I appreciate the effort, but he can't compare with the passion and skill of Henry. I know it's unfair to compare. I'm sure I'm not the same partner now either. Derek and I are like puzzle pieces that go together fine but don't quite fit. You can leave it there if you'd like, but eventually, it will spoil the entire masterpiece. Yes, that's exactly how I'd describe Derek.

Derek is a protector in ways Henry could never even pretend to be. While our sexual feelings toward each other are lukewarm at best, Derek treats me like I am his number one priority. He's always been extremely generous to me, both emotionally and materialistically. I couldn't ask for a better husband. Besides, is it realistic for all of someone's needs to be met by the same person?

Henry and I waited impatiently for over a week for the tracker on the charcoal 4Runner to move. The mystery vehicle was never far from our thoughts. We were just sitting down to dinner one evening when the beeper started chirping. We both jumped up and ran out the door, leaving our Tuscan soup and dinner rolls to get cold and stale. I'd discovered cooking for two people was a lot of fun. It was way better than cooking for one. My countless Food Network tutorials were paying off.

We raced toward the beeping dot, me in the passenger seat navigating as Henry's white knuckles gripped the steering wheel. We'd talked about this moment a million times. There was no plan. There were far too many variables to form a concrete plan. That's why we'd developed such a strong connection. We had to trust each other. There was no other option.

We caught up with the gray SUV just past Frenchman's Bay where we backed off and followed from a short distance. Thankfully traffic through town went smoothly. Sometimes it was hit or miss during foliage season. A few minutes out of town, the car turned left and pulled into one of the most luxurious homes in Bar Harbor. The property was locked and guarded by a solid black gate. Thick pine trees surrounded both sides of the monstrous gate. We couldn't see inside. I snapped pictures with my phone, getting every angle I could, as detailed as possible.

"We'll have to come back," Henry said without missing a beat. "We'll research this place and come back."

"Yes," I concurred like a true accomplice. "We'll figure out a way to get in there."

We drove home in silence, both lost in our own swirling minds.

Seven

I worked diligently through the night while Henry slept. I knew he needed his sleep. So did I, but this was more important. Something about that location had triggered me. I could picture it in my mind back when I was a young child, maybe four or five years old. We'd stopped outside the gate. I could hear my parents in the front seat remarking about the damage caused by the latest hurricane. I remember being aggravated, hungry perhaps. Maybe we'd been on our way to dinner. I don't recall, but I remember sitting there staring at that black gate for a very long time while my parents talked to a man in a uniform. Perhaps a policeman, or a security guard. That was it. That was the only memory I had of the place and apparently,

I'd successfully buried it until now. Odd, because I'd driven by there a zillion times over the years. Somehow, I knew in my gut that my suspicions were correct. I was sure this was where they lived. So sickeningly close. It made sense but it also baffled me at the same time. As it was, I didn't know much, but I knew I had to get into that house. It had to be me. I was their daughter. If things went south, they'd never harm me. Hell, they'd just given me half a million dollars. That was my worth or the house's worth, I suppose. Either way, the fact remained that they would recognize me in a heartbeat. I needed a disguise and a job and pronto. I needed a solid plan before Henry woke up, otherwise, I wasn't sure where his brilliant, yet sketchy mind might lead us.

Suddenly a lightbulb clicked in my brain, and I started researching cleaning companies in the area. I could be a maid, or better yet, a nanny. But again, would they recognize me? Henry would most likely be recognizable too. If they had his daughter, chances were good they researched him. My guess was my parents didn't do much of anything without sufficient background checks. Maybe I could hire staff and create my own business. I could rig up uniforms with cameras. No, I couldn't do that. I couldn't chance other people getting hurt and I didn't have time for all that. The truth is, I didn't know what to do. I had to fix this. I had to. For Henry.

As he slept, I dressed in black leggings and a black hooded sweatshirt. I tied my hair back in a tight ponytail and swirled it around so I could coil it up on top of my head. I tiptoed to the hall closet and grabbed Henry's bag. I quickly removed a black ski cap and a tiny nickel-plated pistol. I grabbed a handful of ammo and zipped the bag shut. Would I kill for Henry? Could I spend the rest of my life in jail for Henry? Maybe they wouldn't throw me in jail. Maybe I could prove I had innocent motives. I took a deep breath and walked out into the darkness of the wee morning.

I drove toward Frenchman's Bay and kept driving past the big black gate. I parked along the tree line half a mile from the property. I tucked the gun into my waistband, grabbed the binoculars out of the glove compartment, and started my hike up the side of the steep incline leading back to the location in question. When I reached the top of the ridge looking down on the mystery house, I lay on the ground and brought the binoculars to my eyes.

Occasionally, there are moments in life you wish you could take back. Defining moments that end up becoming a permanent part of who we are, more so than we ever thought possible. Had I known what I would see on the other end of Henry's cheap binoculars, I'm sure I still would have completed my mission, but I would have liked a warning—a chance to brace myself. Instead, I looked through the lenses at the only light on in the entire mansion and I saw my parents snuggled in bed with the most adorable little redheaded girl. They were reading her a bedtime story. My dad held the book and I watched, stunned, as his lips moved. My mother brushed her hand slowly over the girl's curls, presumably trying to comfort her back to sleep. I stared, unable to look away. In one brief second, I'd seen something so foreign, so unimaginable to me. And it wasn't the fact that it was indeed my parents with Suzie, it was what they were doing, how they were being. It looked like they loved this girl. Suzie. Henry's Suzie. They could steal her and love her, but they couldn't love me. Tears formed in my eyes and streamed down my face until I no longer could see anything but a blurry image of a life that clearly wasn't mine.

I slithered slowly back down the embankment. I knew what I needed to do now. There was no escaping it. I drove home in silence like a zombie. I walked inside and gently woke Henry.

"She's there," I said in monotone.

"Where?" he said as he sat up yawning and rubbing his eyes.

"At the house with the gate. She's there with my parents." I stared ahead while I spoke, looking at nothing but the darkness that had now seeped into my soul.

"How do you know?" He sat up straighter.

"I went there."

"When?"

"Just now." I stood up and motioned at my attire.

"How did you get in?" he asked.

"I didn't. I hiked up through the woods and watched from the top of the hill. She's there. She's with them. They love her."

"What do you mean?" He pushed for more details.

"They were reading her a bedtime story. It was all very picturesque." I sounded more jealous than I thought I felt.

He held his hand out to me but I didn't take it. I couldn't go to him. In that instance, I hated him. If he hadn't come along with his insane theories and crippling dependencies, I would never have known anything about this. I'd never know my parents were kidnappers, psychotic criminals as it appeared. Capable of loving their victim but not their daughter.

"Have you thought about what happens after this, Henry?" I turned toward the window, my back to him as I spoke. "Have you thought about what you're going to do?"

"Do with what?" He was less awake than I thought.

"When you get Suzie back, what is your plan with me?" My voice held no emotion; its emptiness made me shiver.

"Ryan," he stood behind me now, his arms wrapped around my midsection trying to comfort me. His body froze when he felt the gun in my hoodie pocket. He spun me around and retrieved the weapon. He stared at me, not saying a word.

"I need to know the plan," I repeated, looking him dead in the eyes. "I'm prepared to kill for you. What are you prepared to do for me?"

"I'd never ask you to do that." He put the gun on the nightstand.

"Are you kidding?" I laughed a bit too aggressively. "You'd never ask me to do that?"

"Ryan, I..." He started to explain but I interrupted him.

"What do you think all of this is, Henry? How did you think this was going to end?" I was pacing the bedroom now. I pulled my hoodie off and threw it into the armchair in the corner of the room. Bullets rained down over the hardwood floor as they escaped the sweatshirt pocket.

"You can't put yourself in harm's way for me," he seethed. His voice teetered between anger and concern.

"Harm's way?" I chuckled. I went into the bathroom and tossed cool water on my face. I grabbed the hand towel and sat on the arm of the chair. "How did you think this was going to end, Henry?" I repeated.

"Why does it have to end?" He stood in front of me and tipped my chin up with one slender finger. "I thought you said you'd stay."

"Suzie will hate me. My parents abducted her." I blinked back unbidden tears.

"She doesn't know that," he scoffed. "Look," I stiffened at his tone. He made me feel ridiculously pretentious. "Let's just get through this and see where we land on the other side." He pulled me up to stand in front of him and when he tried to kiss me I turned my head away. His lips felt unwanted on my cheek. I could feel his erection against my body. It irritated me. Henry used sex like a Band-Aid. Like it would mend any issue we were dealing with. Usually, it did. But as dawn slowly peered in our windows, I knew this issue was unfixable. I walked past him and made my way to the kitchen to make coffee.

I couldn't get the beautiful book-reading bedtime scene out of my head. Suzie looked so happy there, living my lost childhood. She looked like she knew what home felt like. Here I was more than double her age, and I didn't know what home felt like. I couldn't be jealous. Could I? Jealous of this kidnapped little girl who watched her mother get murdered in front of her? They were giving her an amazing life; far better than what Henry could afford. The thought made me cringe. How could they love her and not me?

"I'm sorry for what this is doing to you," Henry had walked up behind me at the coffee pot and was gathering my long brown hair into one hand. With his other hand, he turned my face to his. "And I am yours, Ryan. Forever. I'm willing to do anything to prove that to you."

He kissed me and kept kissing a trail of wet kisses down my neck. So wet. And then I realized the wetness was tears. My tears. They trailed after him, a reflection of what, I'm not sure. My relief and happiness at his answer, though slow in coming? Or the desperate satisfaction that came from feeling something other than betrayal? I turned into his arms and clung to him as if he were my last breath. I didn't dare let go. I cried harder than I'd cried in my entire life. My tears were the tears of only one thing: pain. It stabbed through me with the sure precision of a freshly sharpened blade.

***

Orange chocolate Milano cookies taste like Christmas. When I was growing up, every Christmas our groundskeeper, Marcus, would give me a bag of orange chocolate Milano cookies. Marcus was a tender soul, who hailed here from Jamaica in search of steadier income. He kept everything outside neat and perfectly luscious. He took care of the gardens, kept up on the maintenance, and plowed and sanded the driveway during the brutal winter months. No matter what job he was doing, Marcus gave one hundred percent effort, but I always saw sadness in his eyes. Perhaps he pitied me. Perhaps he was sad and lonely in his own life. He was one of the few people I missed the most now, as an adult.

I looked out the window of the hotel lobby as I waited for Derek to check out and I bit into an orange chocolate Milano cookie. I thought to myself about how much my life had changed since my youth and Marcus. Since my days before Henry, and after. Now I am a real grownup. Now I have a husband and a successful career as a litigator. Derek and I own a gorgeous house together in Denver. I could have bought it on my own. I was doing well. I didn't *need* anyone in my life, not like I did back then. Back when I needed Henry to breathe for me.

When he held me in the kitchen that day, it was all I could do to breathe. I'd never experienced a panic attack before, but I imagine that's what happened to me. I felt like my entire world was crumbling, disintegrating around me under the weight of my soul-crushing discovery. Henry held me and did his best to console my breaking spirit. I felt so abandoned. So unwanted. I felt like I was in a world I wasn't supposed to be in. Logically speaking, it didn't make sense for me to blame Henry for my misfortune. It was out of his control too and certainly not his fault. I knew that. It's what allowed me to let him in, to not push him away. We would be bonded together forever due to this. I just had to get a hold of myself so we could take care of business. We needed to get Suzie back. Beyond that, I didn't know. I just didn't know.

Were we all victims of circumstance? Me, Henry, Suzie, Richard, and Diane? What triggered people to steal children? To murder mothers? Did they do it themselves? Did my dad murder Catherine? Or did their associate do it? And beyond all that, how was I supposed to retaliate without becoming like them? My soul was shredded inside my shell. I was wise enough to know you can't choose your parents; that's another indisputable fact of life. You can learn from them, from their failures and successes. You can draw lines in the sand. Thick distinct lines; things you swear you'll never do, ways you vouch to be different and better. You can grow past them, realizing their goals and expectations are not yours and that's okay. You can love them regardless, or not at all. The power comes in knowing it's your choice. I didn't have any reason to love my parents. I appreciated the necessities they gave me in life, but I could have gotten those same necessities at a homeless shelter.

"Let's go back," I said, drying my tears.

"Maybe we shouldn't," Henry nodded his head as he said the words.

"What?" I snarled.

"Well, I mean, if she's not hurt. If she's happy there..."

"Are you kidding me?" I protested angrily. "After everything we've been through? Henry, we are so close! She's your daughter, not theirs!"

"I'm just saying, I don't want anyone to get hurt."

"It's too late for that." I stared out the window into the cool fall day. Suddenly, I had a terrific idea. "Henry, sweetheart," I changed my tone to a more inviting octave. "Tonight, you're going to meet my parents."

"I am?" Henry chuckled.

"Yes, sir. It's about time I introduced you to them."

"And how are we going to do this?" he asked.

"We're just going to stop by."

"Stop by, where?"

"Their house. The place with the gate."

"Just stop by? Have you ever done that with them, ever?" He raised one eyebrow at my ridiculous plan."

I didn't need to search my mind for an answer. I'd never popped in on them. Hell, until now I didn't even have their address. I'd never surprised them at work, or a hotel, or even a restaurant. This would be a first.

"I have not," I admitted. "But I am their daughter, whether or not they like it. I should be able to stop by. Especially if I'm introducing them to my fiancé." I said the last word gingerly as I batted my red, irritated-from-crying eyes at him.

"But we're not..." he started.

"Really, Henry? Now is not the time to worry about logistics. They don't know we're not."

"We could be." He paralyzed me with his eyes. They were piercing through me, branding me to him. He stepped forward and took my hands in his. "You asked me what I was willing to do for you. Let me prove it to you for the rest of our lives. Marry me, Ryan."

His words were more of a command than a question. I nodded. I could be a good stepmom to sweet Suzie. I would spend the rest of my life making up for what my parents did to her.

"It's settled then," I let out a deep breath. "Tonight, we'll go meet Richard and Diane."

Henry and I managed to nap most of the day. When we woke, the sun was starting to set. Dusk crept in along the Maine shoreline like a black panther stalking its unsuspecting prey. Our prey this evening resided in a house I'd never entered. I had no idea what to expect when we got inside *if* we got inside, but we had to try. Suzie needed us.

Henry wore nice crisp khaki pants and a tropical button-up shirt. His boat shoes completed the ensemble, portraying him as more a tourist than a true coastal native. There were a lot of tourists this time of year. One last hurrah before snow blanketed our little island, sending almost everyone into hibernation until spring.

We stepped on red, orange, and yellow fallen leaves as we walked to the car. They stuck to the wet ground, lifeless. It must have showered while we were sleeping. I wore a maroon form-fitting dress. It was my favorite casual dress, made of cotton, and went great with a sweater. I tossed my sweater in the back seat. It landed on top of Henry's duffel bag. I wished I could forget the real reason for this night out. I wanted with all my heart to just be taking my fiancé to meet my parents, a small but significant step in any normal person's journey. My journey was not normal. Not in the least.

"Wait," I said as we rounded the corner before the bay. "Pull over."

"What is it?" Henry asked, concerned as he pulled the car to the side of the road.

"There's a shipping container. It's out back. It's green. It blends in with the trees. I don't know why I'm only now remembering it." I massaged my temples with both hands.

"A big one?" Henry prodded me for more information.

"I don't know," I snapped. "This just barely came back to me, just now!"

"It's okay, it's okay," he touched my arm. "We can, um, go up the bank to where you were. You can show me."

"No, no," I shook my head. "We need to do this now. It's more proof of their guilt."

Henry slowly started driving again. I could feel him watching me, probably wondering if I was going to blow this whole operation sky-high. From his perspective, I could see how he'd think I was a risky asset. We pulled up to the mysterious black gate and I leaned over Henry to talk into the intercom.

"Smith Residence, who may I say is approaching?"

"Their daughter," I cleared my throat. "Ryan." My last name was not Smith. I chuckled at their arrogance.

"Please hold," the other end clicked. I rolled my eyes and Henry squeezed my arm reassuringly.

"Hello," the voice came back on. "They don't have a daughter named Ryan. Please move along." The male voice sounded annoyed. I'm sure this happens a lot, pranksters trying to get into rich properties.

"Yes, they do," I pressed further. "Please tell Richard and Diane I want to introduce them to my fiancé, that's all."

"Please hold."

Silence. Long, loud silence. Nothing. I was sure I'd blown our only chance to gain access to this place.

"Let's just go," I told Henry. We started backing away. We were about to pull onto the main road when the gate opened, and Richard and Diane stepped through. "Wait," I told Henry for the second time this evening. "That's them."

He stopped and we sat in the car as my beloved parents approached.

"Darling!" My mother opened the passenger side door and hugged me immediately. I froze. I'd rather be strip-searched by the TSA. Did she have a weapon on her person? I'd gone my entire life without a hug from this woman. I felt molested now, as her body pressed up against mine. "It's so nice to see you! We are headed out for the evening, otherwise, we'd invite you up!" Her voice was a pitch I'd never heard before. It scratched at my eardrums. Richard stood silent at her side. I could only see his legs and shiny shoes from my angle in the car.

"This is, um, Henry, my fiancé." I grabbed his hand and held on for dear life. Henry opened his mouth to speak but Diane cut him off.

"So, you need money for the wedding. Of course!" she clucked. "Is that why you're here?" Out of the corner of my eye, I could see Richard reaching into his pocket. He brought out a money clip fat with bills.

"Um, no," I said more meekly than I liked. "I just wanted you to meet him."

"Well here," she said and handed me Richard's entire money clip. "We're so happy you're happy!"

"I don't need…" I started to refuse when Richard reached into his pocket and retrieved a second money clip even fatter than the first one.

"And please, don't return," he whispered in my ear as he tossed the money onto my lap.

"Very nice to meet you both," Henry lied. "We should go, huh babe?" He patted my hand. I didn't move. I didn't speak. I felt frozen, like maybe I'd been stabbed with one of those needles that made you unable to move but all your senses still worked fine. My mother closed my car door and backed up.

As we drove away, the money clips slipped off my lap and landed at my feet. I stared down at them aimlessly. Diane had seemed nice at first. I earnestly wanted to believe she was being genuine, that she was happy to see me. But Richard's words echoed in my brain, reverberating through my body like an earthquake's aftershock. *Please don't return.* I shivered.

"That wasn't the plan," I said angrily. My voice was accusatory beyond measure like I thought everything going wrong in my life was Henry's fault.

"Sometimes you have to throw the plan out," he replied softly.

"We can't. We can't give up." I cleared my throat and reached down to pick up the two money clips. "However, we can let them fund our mission." The clips were plain chrome. I was expecting to see fancy calligraphed initials but there were none. Made sense, I guess, if you're trying to keep a low profile. Richard's angry voice was still ringing in my ears. "We have to go back," I whispered. "They can't get away with this."

"They won't." Henry rested his hand on my trembling thigh. "We need a real plan. Not that your idea wasn't good, it was. And I'm so appreciative of your effort, but this is going to be a lot harder than we thought. We need some time to brainstorm what to do."

"We need to go back," I said firmly. "We need to go in there and get Suzie. They don't know we know about her. We can use that to our advantage."

"How do you suggest we get inside?" he asked.

"We need to watch the property, without watching the property." I sat up taller in my seat.

"I have game cameras." Henry winked at me. "We can set them up in the trees across the street so we can watch the entrance.

"Perfect!" I clapped excitedly. "We can study them. See when they come and go. Maybe we can sneak in with a trash truck or something."

"Yes! Baby, I love you!" Henry felt the words as he said them. I could tell.

"I love you too," I squeezed his hand in mine. "We will get her back."

Eight

Two weeks later, after countless hours watching the camera footage, we were no further ahead than we had been. In fact, we felt further behind. Yes, we knew where Suzie was, but it felt a million times worse knowing she was just down the street and we couldn't get to her. The only peace we could find was that she appeared to be healthy and happy. As two weeks turned to three, both Henry and I were filled to the brim with restlessness and irritability. One evening we looked at each other, defeat threatening to swallow us whole. Suddenly, I jumped up from the chair I'd been lounging in.

"Come on, let's go over there. We can put all black on and hike up the backside like I did before. We can watch and scout. Maybe we can find something to help us or give us a clue. It's worth a shot."

"Okay," he agreed. "I can't sit here like this much longer either."

Sometimes I look back on how fragile I was back then. How needy and broken I was. How I was still very much a dependent, yet I had no one to depend on. I've heard it said eighteen is a tender age and I would have to agree. I felt everything so much deeper than everyone else. I was sure of it. Not just love and all the warm fuzzy feelings. Abandonment fit like a glove even though I knew I was never truly abandoned. My needs were always met. Richard and Diane threw money at me like candy thrown from a hay-lined float in a parade on a hot sunny summer day. What I wouldn't give to have even one memory of a bedtime story...

Henry and I bundled up and ventured to the gated house. Winter was only a couple weeks away now and the days were shorter than ever. Darkness blanketed us.

"Don't shoot unless you absolutely have to," he ordered as he handed me a gun. Its weight felt soothing in my hand. I took a deep breath and exhaled slowly. "I love you, Ryan," he whispered.

"I love you. Now let's go get your daughter back." I clinked my weapon to his as if they were shot glasses.

As we hiked toward the house in the same direction I'd taken before, I suddenly wasn't scared of tomorrow or of what might happen after. Henry and I clicked. We'd clicked from the moment we met. I had no doubt we'd settle into a nice little life together with Suzie and I couldn't wait to make that happen.

We approached the crest of the hill and sank on our bellies to observe. There were no lights on. Perhaps they had dinner plans out again. Perfect. Maybe we could sneak inside and snoop around.

"I don't think they're home," I whispered to Henry.

Just then car lights shone brightly from the direction of the driveway. We instinctively crouched down lower. I popped my head back up to survey our surroundings and the first thing I noticed was what the headlights illuminated in the distance.

Far across the large grassy yard, at the edge of the tree line was a dark green, or gray, storage container. I couldn't quite tell the color from my angle.

"Look!" I flailed my hand at Henry to get his attention. "Look at the end of the headlights. It's the shipping container!" As I said the words, the headlights shut off and we heard car doors shutting.

"They're home now," Henry stated the obvious.

"We have to get down there. We have to look at that container."

"They just got home. We should wait a bit," Henry directed.

"Let's walk around the edge of the property, through those trees." I pointed to my right.

"Okay," he agreed.

We started making our way through the woods, creating a big loop around the long rectangular object. Branches crackled under our weight in the forest. The moonlight helped illuminate the night and soon we were at our destination, staring at the shipping container as if we could see through it somehow. I couldn't tell if it was new or not. I thought it looked newer, only because most older containers are orange and rusty. Perhaps they painted this one.

"We have to go check it out," I said to Henry and started walking toward it.

"We need to make a plan," Henry tugged on my hood, stopping me in my tracks.

"You said it yourself; sometimes you have to throw the plan out." I reminded him of his most beloved statement.

"I just... We need to be careful." His voice was scolding.

"I want her back as much as you do," I stood up taller as I pleaded my case.

"Do you?" Henry's question took me off guard. "Or do you just want vengeance?"

"Excuse me?" I hissed.

"I'm just saying, let's be careful." He backtracked. Now was not the time for a pissing match.

"May I remind you, I was fine with my life before you came along," I snapped angrily.

"Were you?" Henry snapped back. "You didn't seem fine, all alone, at Christmas."

"Well, I was!" I shouted in a failed whisper.

"Shh!" Henry moved closer to me and covered my mouth with his hand. "We're better together, no?" He asked softly into my ear. I could barely hear his words. My body tightened at his intensity. I nodded yes, my mouth wet against his hand. My heart pounded. The tiny hairs on the back of my neck stood up straight. It was then that I knew this would be a night to remember. I wanted Henry more than I wanted anyone or anything else. He released his hand and kissed me briskly.

"I will stay here, by the tree line, while you go peek at the container," I promised.

"No," he shook his head. "You go. I'll wait here. Just be careful. I trust you."

I trust you. No one had ever said that phrase to me. I kissed him happily and started walking toward the container. To my surprise and relief, it was unlocked.

"Pssst!" I called into the woods. "It's unlocked!"

"Really?" Henry was at my side in a flash.

I turned the handle and the door swung open, creaking and moaning in protest.

"Shhh!" I begged. I looked toward the house to see if we'd been spotted but no one seemed to notice. Henry clicked his flashlight on and peered inside.

"It's empty," he said in disbelief. "And clean."

"Clean?" I parroted him.

"Spotless."

"Spotless like someone was just in there with bleach, spotless?" I asked.

"Exactly," Henry sighed, aggravated beyond measure.

"Can I help you find something?" A voice sounded from behind us. I'd looked away for two seconds. Two seconds to peek inside the recently Mr. Cleaned container. Now Richard's voice echoed in my ears.

"No thanks," I turned to face him. "I'm just looking."

"What are you looking for, Ryan?" My father stepped closer to me, both hands in his pockets, chest out, like the arrogant asshole I barely knew.

"You tell me, Dad," I placed an especially sarcastic emphasis on the word 'dad'. "What is so mysterious about this place?"

"There's nothing mysterious here," Richard chirped, tippy-toeing up on his tasseled loafers as he spoke.

"I see." I clasped my hands behind my back and circled him like a detective would. "Why is there a squeaky clean shipping container in your backyard? Surely you don't need the storage, what with your oversized garage and all."

"I'm turning it into a tiny home," he chuckled. "What else would you like to know?"

"Richard?" a familiar voice called from behind him. "Richard, what is it?"

"Nothing, Diane. Go back in the house," he directed.

"It's not nothing, Richard. You're talking to someone." She pushed past him and stood face to face with me, the daughter she didn't want.

"Ryan, what on Earth?" she gasped. "What are you doing here?"

"What am I doing here? What are you doing here?" I flipped the question back onto her.

"What are you talking about?" She looked confused.

What happened next changed my life forever. Before I knew what was going on, a short blob of red curly hair ran into our circle and clung to Diane's leg.

"Suzie, sweetheart, go back inside," Diane chastised her. She clung tighter to my mother, a woman I couldn't imagine hugging. At the sound of Suzie's name, Henry emerged from the shipping container. He stood in front of it, his eyes not leaving the child.

"Suzie?" He had tears in his throat. "Suzie, it's Dad!"

Horrified, Diane scooped Suzie up into her arms.

"What are you talking about?" Richard snapped haughtily.

"Have you always had her?" I asked, sneering.

"We adopted her," my mother answered for him. "Last year."

"You didn't adopt her!" I screamed. "You stole her!"

"That is quite enough!" Richard yelled back.

"She is my daughter," Henry stepped forward. "You killed her mother and you took her." His teeth were gritted together so tightly I was sure they would crack under the strain.

"No." My mother started backing up slowly with Suzie in her arms. I swung out wide and positioned myself behind her, facing the shipping container. I had her trapped.

"Suzie, sweetheart..." Henry got down on one knee, pleading with his daughter to recognize him. Suzie kept her eyes glued shut, her hands over her ears. My heart broke for her. Surely, she was remembering her mother's death, being traumatized all over again. Richard stood helplessly frozen in the same spot he'd been in. Diane called the shots.

"I have one question." I stepped closer to the woman who was supposed to be my mom. "Why did you want her, but not me?" My eyes felt like blades of steel, cold, yet searing hot at the same time.

"It's not like that, Ryan." My mother's voice cracked as she talked. "Lord knows I've made a million mistakes in this life, but you were always cared for."

"Cared for, yes," I admitted. "But never loved."

"I'm so sorry," Diane cried what I was sure were fake tears. She set Suzie down on the grass. "Go to Daddy, honey," she instructed.

Suzie didn't move at first but then she took two or three steps and stopped. She looked at Richard and Henry and then back at Richard.

"Suzie, honey, it's me! It's Daddy!" Henry tried to smile. Suzie looked at Richard with solemn eyes and then ran in Henry's direction.

"No!" Diane yelled and started running towards her. In that instant, I didn't think. I just reacted. My protective instincts clicked into overdrive and I pulled the gun out of my waistband.

"No!" I heard Henry yell but it was too late. I'd already pulled the trigger, aiming at my mother. Without thinking twice or even once, for that matter, I wanted her dead. I wanted Suzie safe. I heard the loud cling as the bullet ricocheted off the side of the shipping container. Then everyone was screaming, huddled on the ground over a pile of orange curly hair. Suzie's lifeless body lay still on the grass. Her parents, all three of them, desperately tried to revive her.

I stood there, holding the murder weapon, in shock at what had just happened. It all transpired so quickly. So effortlessly. I dropped the now super heavy gun in the grass and I slowly backed away until I could turn and run. I ran back to the car where I climbed inside and retrieved my wallet. On second thought, I got inside and buckled my seatbelt. I pulled out onto the road and I drove. I drove until I couldn't drive any longer. I drove all night long. I stopped at a truck stop as dawn approached and got a few hours of sleep before continuing my travels.

The next day, just north of Myrtle Beach, I decided I should form a new plan or at least have a destination in mind. I decided to aim for Charleston and started thinking about what kind of job I wanted. I had plenty of money but not nearly enough peace of mind. If I didn't get a job I would surely drive myself crazy sitting around alone all the time. Lord knows I had plenty to think about. Plenty to desperately try to forget.

I rented a little cottage on the beach. It was on the outskirts of what I'm sure was a plantation here in the deep south. This place held history. It had meaning. You could feel it in the air. The week after I settled in, I decided to go to the local community college and see what they offered. That was when I began my journey into criminal justice. I needed to learn how to be a better investigator. There had to have been something I missed all along in the case of Richard and Diane. They were the real criminals.

Henry never came up again. I left Bar Harbor that night and I never spoke of the happenings there. Not to anyone. Not even Derek. I met Derek in the college food court one rainy spring day. Derek was an architecture major. He was refreshingly different in more ways than I could numerate. He was tall, dark, and beautiful, much like myself, and I jumped headfirst into the necessary distraction he became.

I waited for months, my breath catching in my throat at every phone call, every knock on my door. No one ever came with handcuffs to arrest me for Suzie's murder. I read her obituary in the paper one Sunday morning while I sat on my porch swing watching the ocean.

They must have reconciled, the three of them, and decided not to press charges. I mean, whose fault was it anyway? I pulled the trigger but who *really* killed Suzie? Her loving captures or her unstable father? Maybe it was my mistrust, my insurmountable jealousy, or my unchecked anger. The kind of anger you can't control even a little bit. The kind of anger where you feel like you're outside your body looking in. It's a terrifying place to be, void of all reason and logic.

Derek nursed me back to life without even knowing I was wounded. He was such a breath of fresh air. When we had free time we'd travel and look at all sorts of rich architecture. From Barcelona and Athens to our backyard in

Charleston and down to New Orleans, there were so many spectacular buildings to discover. They were more than buildings to Derek. They held stories. His passion for historical structures was transformative to him. I watched him as the years went by, as we both grew and our lives slowly started weaving together. I watched him become exactly like the buildings he admired; strong, sure, and distinguished. Buildings don't change the way people or even scenery do. Buildings remain the same, unwavering over time. To make something like that, so solid and impressive, commanding the attention of those around it, that was Derek's dream and I happily followed after him, slowly picking away at my career as we traveled.

One day I spotted a newly printed flier of a missing girl with red hair and I knew I couldn't hide any longer. The picture, while I knew it wasn't Suzie, reminded me of all the missing girls. The ones Henry and I never found, and all the other countless missings boys and girls, those missing and those unnoticed. I knew I had to do more. I stopped traveling with Derek and I began dedicating every second I could to bringing families back together. I got my degree in criminal profiling and while Derek was beyond supportive of my work, I could see our lives slowly unraveling from each other.

We married the Christmas after graduation. I did my best to smile; never telling Derek Christmas was my least favorite time of year. Derek brought sparkle to my life, consistency, and care: things I'd never known before. Even now, as we've become more roommates than spouses, I am forever grateful for Derek. It's why I don't mind coming with him to places like Newark.

I never went back to Bar Harbor, not even after Richard and Diane died in a freak house fire a few years later. I didn't owe them anything. They owed me my innocence and childhood, not to mention my sanity. They owed me unpayable debts. When they passed, I wasn't mentioned in the obituary, or will, or estate. I died the day I killed their chosen daughter.

Slowly I surrendered all my unanswered questions to the stars. Things that didn't matter anymore. Things that did matter but I knew I'd never resolve. I tried not to think of that life; the regrets, the mistakes, and the lessons that were forever seared into my soul. Those are the things that stick with you over the years. It's not what I did that haunted me but rather what I didn't do. I should have taken Suzie, somehow and fled with her. We could have started our own story, safely tucked away from Richard and Diane and Henry. I should have gone to the police, instead of believing Henry's tall tales. I should have known better so many times, but I didn't. I believed Henry because I wanted to believe Henry. Henry, though perhaps delusional at times, had shown me what living was all about. He showed me the passion that comes with loving people enough to do anything for their safety and happiness. Had things gone differently that fatal night, I don't doubt that Henry, Suzie, and I would have made an incredible family. It's what I wanted so badly. It's what Henry wanted. It just wasn't in the cards. Still, everywhere I go, even to this day, if I hear Henry's name, I get goosebumps and my eyes wander even though I beg them not to.

Nine

On the plane ride home from Newark, Derek told me he wanted a divorce. He said he met someone else. It was nothing personal against me. He still loved me and wanted me to be happy, but his heart was elsewhere. I understood what he was saying because I'd felt the same way since the beginning. Derek was comfortable, like my favorite fleece sweater, but my heart was miles and miles from our home.

When we stopped for our layover in Chicago, I was the last one off the plane. I sat still in my seat as all the passengers deplaned. I knew what I had to do. I ran to catch up with Derek inside the terminal and I told him I was going home to Maine.

"Are you sure? Do you want me to come with you?" he asked with concern in his voice.

"No, I'm fine, thank you. I need to go alone. There's someone I need to see." I winked at my soon-to-be ex-husband, yet another chapter ended. "Thank you for everything, Derek." With that, I kissed him on the cheek, turned, and walked to the ticket counter to exchange my ticket for one to Bangor, Maine.

I had a five-hour layover before my flight. Not long enough to bother leaving the airport. I didn't know my way around and I couldn't think of one single thing in Chicago that would be worth having to go through TSA again. I welcomed the stillness of simply sitting and staring out the window watching airplanes come and go. People are always so busy. Everyone is in a rush. You don't see many people smiling in airports. There's always another destination and you can never get there fast enough.

After two hours of staring out the smudgy windows, I decided I needed a drink. I headed to the nearest restaurant, straying only a few shops away from my gate. I made my way toward the bar, past the booths and through the tables, and as I did my skin prickled, tightening like a raisin. I shivered and wiped my arms, dropping my tote bag to the floor at my feet. A man approached and bent down to pick up my spilled items. When he stood back up, I couldn't believe my eyes. Did I manifest him? Henry stood in front of me. He was older, grayer, and softer than I remembered. Upon first glance, he looked nice, mellow even. I blinked.

"Ryan?" I heard him ask in astonishment.

I couldn't speak. Here I was, twenty years older, and I still felt like that crazy smitten young woman standing in front of the shop window on Main Street. I inched one finger out and poked his arm to see if he was real. I'd certainly been thinking of him this weekend, as my marriage disintegrated. That is why I was here, after all, waiting for my solo trip to Bangor. In search of what, I'm not sure. Perhaps I didn't need to search anymore. Maybe my searching days were gone.

"H...Henry," I stuttered. My legs felt weak, and I was thankful he'd pulled me into a warm embrace. Warmer than I deserved after killing his daughter. In a flash, the last twenty years disappeared, and I was back in Richard and Diane's yard, dropping the gun and backing away slowly. This time I backed into another patron.

"Wait," Henry held onto my hand as I tried to back away. This wasn't what I expected if I expected anything at all. This was a terrible idea! I killed Suzie. It was an accident, of course, but still. How could he want to hug me?

"Wait, please," he begged. "Let me talk to you, just for a moment."

His eyes were different, once I let myself look into them. They were more sincere than I remembered. He was humble like the years had turned him into someone else completely. One's wife and daughter being murdered was sure to do that to a person. I let him lead me to a bar stool where he secured my luggage under my seat.

"So where are you headed?" He attempted to make small talk after I ordered a shot of tequila.

"Henry, I...geez, I don't even know what to say to you." I stared at him. The bartender refilled my shot glass. I didn't even have to ask him to. Perceptive.

"I've thought about this moment a million times," Henry said.

My eyes fell to the bar top. It was wooden, cheap, what you'd expect to find in an airport lounge. There were cracks in the surface, scars of a tortured existence.

"Henry, I..." I continued but he quickly interrupted me.

"Please don't say you're sorry." He grabbed my hand. I wanted to pull it away, but I couldn't figure out how to. It was like my brain was completely disconnected from my body. "Ryan, it wasn't your fault. It was my fault. Jesus, you were just a kid and I put so much pressure on you. I...I don't know what I was thinking. I was in a horrible place."

"You were grieving your wife," I cut in, finally able to function. "And because of me, you had to grieve your daughter too. I'll forever be sorry for that."

"You were my light in an impenetrable darkness," he kissed my hand. "Thank you, Ryan. And please know I don't blame you for anything."

I looked at him. He was night and day different from the Henry I knew. He seemed to be almost embarrassed of the past. I wasn't. Other than my murdering Suzie, I loved my time with Henry. I wasn't embarrassed or upset about it in the least. He had made me feel, well, grown up. Needed.

"So where are you headed? You're traveling light." He motioned to my single tote bag.

"Oh yes, well, I was headed home from a work weekend, and I decided to make a last-minute detour."

"I see. And, where's home for you now?" He was still holding my hand as he spoke, but I pretended not to notice.

"That's...um...currently up in the air." I tipped back another tequila shot.

"You're married," he stated flatly, pointing to my ring finger.

"Very recently divorced. Well, divorcing," I nodded.

"Oh, I'm sorry," he lied.

"It's fine," I laughed. "It's amicable. He's a good man."

"Then why the split?" He eyed me intently. His eyes sparkled in a way I'd never seen them sparkle before. He seemed happy. I couldn't remember ever seeing him happy. I smiled at him a moment before answering his question.

"Lack of passion, I'd say." I reached past him slowly, my breast caressing his arm as I stretched to get the tiny tent menu.

"I could have reached that for you," he said as I settled back into my seat.

"I know," I winked.

"Wow, you're even more gorgeous now than you were then," he admired me.

"You're not aging too bad yourself," I smiled at him again.

"So you're not going to tell me where you're headed?" He tipped his head to one side in a cute manner.

"Nope," I paused to order a burger and fries. "Where are you headed?"

"Vegas," he replied. "I've developed quite a knack for the craps table."

"I'm sure you have," I chuckled at him. Still a gambler, all these years later. He'd gambled with me and scarred me for life. Suddenly, I felt irritated.

"What do you do for work?" He asked, not yet catching on to my mood change.

"Excuse me, sir," I pointed at the bartender. "Can you please cancel my order? I...I can't stay."

"Why?" Henry said, alarmed. "Why can't you stay?"

"I...I can't," I stammered. "I can't do this with you. You...you have no idea how much you sucked me in back then. How much you controlled me. You...you...you used me, Henry. You trained me to be how you wanted me to be and I...I was more than gullible enough to actually enjoy you!" I took a deep breath and clawed my fingers through my hair. "You fucked up my entire life! I haven't been able to have kids. I haven't been able to love anyone. Between you and my parents, I..."

"I killed your parents." He all but whispered the words. I looked around to see if anyone heard him, but no one seemed to care.

"You did?" I sat still in my chair, like if I moved even an inch this moment would dissipate.

"I did. I...I'm not sorry." His voice had turned monotone now.

"Good," I sighed with relief. Real relief, a feeling I hadn't felt in ages. "I was hoping it was you."

"I couldn't let them get away with what they did. To you, to Suzie and Catherine, to God-only-knows how many other girls."

"Nothing ever came of all that? Of all the other missing girls?" I asked.

"No," he shook his head sadly. "But your parents got what was coming to them and since then there haven't been any more kidnappings or missing girls or anything like that."

"Good," I said again.

"Are you staying or going?" The bartender stood in front of me with his tablet.

"I'm staying," I replied. I smiled shyly at Henry.

"Make that two burgers and fries," he ordered, smiling back at me.

Henry and I spent the next couple of hours catching up. He told me my parents refused to press charges against him because they knew he knew they killed Catherine. They'd all end up in jail together, so that was silly. Henry waited long enough so he thought they'd forgotten about him and Suzie and Catherine, and then he torched their house in the middle of the night. It was a perfect death, grasping for breath until their lungs filled with soot and despair. Henry had cleverly disabled the big black gate so it wouldn't open, the access to their fortress of lies, so the fire department had a hard time accessing the property. By the time they got through, the entire house was up in flames. Even the adjacent garage was a complete loss.

I felt a certain vindication, like a wrong had finally been righted. I looked down at my watch. My plane was boarding.

"Oh, I have to go or I'm going to miss my flight." I stood up quickly. Henry and I had exchanged numbers so I could contact him if I ever wanted to. I felt good as if the last few hours had helped me find a missing puzzle piece or two.

Henry stood up and we held each other. We'd both lost track of time and now we had to hurry to our gates. We started in the same direction, and I darted into the ladies' room. I had to pee, and I wanted to avoid any other goodbyes. I felt like I was withering inside like he was my water and sunshine, and without him, I'd surely perish. I gazed into the mirror, in shock at what had just happened. By the time I reached my gate, they were starting to shut the door. I ran and snuck in, just in time. The attendants were very irritated as they checked my ticket and shooed me along.

I always liked the middle of the plane best. The exit row seats had the most legroom, and my body appreciated the extra space to stretch out. When I got to my seat, it was already taken.

"Miss, you're late. We gave your seat to someone else and already conducted our exit-row speech. There's a free seat in the back."

"Oh, free?" I perked up. "Perfect because I paid extra for that one."

"Well, not free. Empty." She corrected herself.

"I see," I rolled my eyes at her and continued my way to the back of the plane. I squeezed my tote under the middle seat and plopped myself between two gentlemen, not looking at either of them while I searched for my seatbelt.

"Oh, excuse me," I said as I pulled my buckle out from under the man sitting near the window.

"No problem," he said. He sounded like he was trying not to laugh and when I looked up to see what was so funny, he was not a stranger at all.

"You lied!" I accused Henry, my mouth dropping open.

"So did you," he elbowed me playfully.

"I didn't lie," I defended myself. "I didn't say."

"Uh-huh," he chuckled. "Why are you going to Maine?"

"Why are you going to Maine?" I cross-examined.

"I still live there," he said, the smile fading from his face.

"Really? After all this time?" I was surprised.

"What can I say? I guess I always hoped you'd come back someday." His eyes held mine steadily before he turned his attention to the runway. We were taking off, bumbling down the pavement, full speed ahead. I laid my head against the back of my seat and closed my eyes. Henry reached over and took my hand in his. Crazy, I thought, how Henry had toppled my life upside down, yet I felt so protected when I was near him. I let my head rest on his shoulder the entire ride to Maine. The entire ride home.

Ten

There is a place called Tranquility where the sky glows bluer and the sun heats warmer, beckoning relaxation and utter bliss. A place where temptation is a beautiful distraction, where touch is a necessity, where all your senses awaken, bidden or otherwise. I watched the clouds interlocking above me. The only sound was the leaves rustling together in the vigorous breeze. My fingers were wet inside my womanhood. I bit my lip, stifling a long low moan, my stress relief coming in waves, quivering through my body much like the breeze.

These are the days I want to last forever. Sometimes I sit and think about my life. About all the choices I've made that have led me here to this very moment. All the arrows and signs and misinterpreted fascinations. The sparkle and shine that draws us in, chases away our fears and creates new fears. The bridges crossed and others broken, never to be repaired. Reparations are a false illusion. If there's one thing I've learned on this journey, that's it.

I lived with Henry for a month before everything changed. He had gone to the store one evening to pick up groceries when I decided to snoop around. He still hadn't touched Suzie's room. It worried me. After twenty years, he hadn't moved on at all. Everything looked the same as it had when I lived here before, only messier. Henry wasn't a very good housekeeper. He didn't have any reason to be. I liked things to be neat and tidy.

When I opened the door to Suzie's room, grief flowed over me. I couldn't believe I killed her. Sweet Suzie. She was just an innocent bystander. I sank to my knees at the side of her bed and I cried. Tears streamed down my cheeks and into Suzie's dark purple comforter. All these years later, I still imagined her to be the daughter I never had. She was the keeper of my emotions. After I killed

Suzie, I never let myself feel very deeply. I kept all my emotions in check, ready to dash and run at a moment's notice. Suzie took my heart with her when she died, crippling my ability to live fully. I cried tears of grief not only for Suzie and Henry but also for myself. For my eighteen-year-old self who was wounded by the stray bullet almost as much as Henry was. Some days I still felt like the whole thing was a bad dream.

I wiped my tears away with the back of my hands and took a deep breath. Something under the sliding closet door caught my attention. I crawled to the closet and slowly slid it open. It was a newspaper article with a picture of Suzie in the heading.

'Missing orphan girl Identified as murdered Bar Harbor redhead.'

I cringed at the sight of the article, gasping for breath as regret threatened to swallow me whole.

I quickly scanned the paper. I thought I'd read all the news articles about Suzie's death.

'After a thoroughly detailed investigation, the coroner has determined the remains of who we previously thought to be Suzie Picard, to be those of Susan Miller. Susan was an orphan from the group home on MDI. She was previously deceased by her parents who were killed in a car accident three years ago. Our condolences go out to anyone who knew Susan. Her life, while lost, will not be forgotten.'

I reread the article, my mouth suddenly dry, my blood surely clotting by the second. My heart raced. Who the fuck was Susan Miller? I looked around Suzie's closet. Totes of old school papers were stacked up in one corner. Snow boots, ice skates, and shoes were on the floor next to the totes. I reached for the top tote, expecting it to be heavy with kindergarten projects, but instead, it was feather-light. I set it on the floor and opened it. It was empty. Images of books and stuffed animals had been printed out and taped to the sides of the clear plastic tote so it appeared as though it was full. I stared at it; my mouth dropped open to the floor. My eyes flew to the remaining totes and a quick investigation led to similar discoveries. Each tote was empty. I threw them across the room as I opened them. Confusion crept through my bones. I eyed the dresser and quickly shuffled through the drawers of little girl clothes. They were all unworn. Brand new clothes laid out before me. I threw them on the floor with the empty totes.

Just then, I heard Henry pull into the driveway. For a second, I thought of running. I could get out the back door before he came in the front. I could escape. In Henry's mind, this last month must have seemed like a honeymoon. We were inseparable, beyond blessed to be back together. We were both excited for the future. A future where we'd remember Suzie and forget about Richard and Diane. But now, in a matter of minutes, everything had changed.

I quickly shut what I thought had been Suzie's bedroom door. I plopped myself on the sofa just as Henry came in with an armful of grocery bags. I jumped up to help him, still reeling from my recent discovery. Everything I knew about Henry was a lie. He didn't even have a daughter. Was Catherine a lie too? My heart thumped in my chest as I put the milk and eggs in the refrigerator. If it wasn't Suzie, who did I kill? Who was Susan? An orphaned girl who thought she had found her forever family? Henry had lied about so many things! Even now, twenty years later, the lies flowed freely from his lips.

I thought of my life and how long I had carried this burden of not only killing Suzie but ruining any chance of happiness for Henry. I'd let that weigh me down for years. It dictated my career and hindered my life beyond reason. If I hadn't met Henry that day, that Christmas Eve so many years ago, my life might have been completely different. Now, as I placed bagels in the breadbox, I felt numb. Numb, restricted, and used. The thought of running and hiding exhausted me. I put the cheese on the counter and turned to face Henry, this skeleton of a stranger. He looked back at me, intently trying to figure out what I was thinking.

"Shit, I forgot to get your ice cream," he tossed an empty bag on the counter.

"Were you ever going to tell me?" I asked, my voice scarily monotone.

"Tell you what? About the ice cream?" He was confused.

"About Susan Miller," I glared at him.

"Susan Miller?" The name made the color instantly drain from his face.

"The little girl I killed," I reminded him.

"Listen, Ryan," he put both hands up as if to calm me down somehow. "No, I probably never would have told you. I didn't want you to feel bad."

"You didn't want me to feel bad?" I repeated each word deliberately.

"No, of course not. It's over and done now. Has been for a long time. And, you know, I keep looking for Suzie every chance I get. In fact, in my spare time, I help manage a group for lost girls and..."

"Oh stop!" I yelled; my volume surprising even myself. "Enough, Henry! No more lies."

"Lies?" he shook his head.

"I know you're lying. There never was a Suzie, was there? You don't have a daughter." It felt good to confront him. Empowering, not to run.

"Ryan, I don't know what you've heard..." he tried to explain.

"Seen. It's what I've seen. Suzie's room is a dollhouse. A fake display. Right here, this whole time! I can't believe I didn't see it before." Henry started to walk towards me, to head to Suzie's room, but I blocked his way. "It's a sick, twisted plot. The totes in the closet are all empty, Henry. They're cleverly portrayed to look full. The clothes are all brand new, never worn. I found the news clipping about Susan on the floor." He stood before me in silence now. His hands shoved into his jean pockets. His eyes were glued to the floor. "Are you a sick and twisted person, Henry?" I whispered the forceful question.

"No," he answered.

"What about all the other girls? What about Catherine?" I kept pressing him.

"She was real. You've seen the pictures. You read the police report."

"I read a lot of things," I fought back tears now. "How could you play me like that? How could you?" I stammered, the reality of the situation slamming into me like a pile of bricks dropped from the sky. "What about Molly? What about the things you did to her? Why?" I was mortified. My skin crawled.

"Ryan, please," he stepped in front of me now and wrapped his arms around my midsection. "We have to move on. We can't let this control our lives anymore."

"We?" I chuckled angrily and wriggled out of his embrace. "Our lives? Henry, you stole my life away from me. I want to know why. Tell me, Henry. Tell me why you did that."

"Revenge," he said matter-of-factly.

"Revenge?" I stepped back. "Revenge for what? What did I ever do to you?"

"Not you, Ryan. I could never hate you. I love you." He raked his fingers through his hair. "It was them. Richard and Diane, your parents. They weren't nice people."

"I know that," I laughed.

"They killed Catherine. I saw them kill Catherine and no one would believe me. No one wanted justice for her. And when I realized you were their daughter, after graduation, I started watching you. I knew I could turn you, manipulate you. I knew you would believe me."

"You barely knew me for one day before you gave me those papers," I said softly.

"I'd been studying you, Ryan. Following you. You know that. I've already confessed to all this."

"You told me they had your daughter," I fought back tears.

"I needed you to be invested in me. I needed you to feel bad for me."

"Feel bad?" I grunted.

"I never thought it would go as far as it did," he continued. "I had no idea they had Susan. When you came home from the park that day, I couldn't tell you the truth. I couldn't lose you. I'm sorry, Ryan. I just...I couldn't...I couldn't stop it once it got going. It's true, lies breed more lies. And it wasn't that I was trying to lie to you, I was just trying to make the story seem believable."

"It wasn't a story to me, Henry," I said, my words barely audible.

We stood in silence, me looking at him, him looking at the floor. Finally, I walked to the counter and picked up my wallet and cell phone. I kept my back to him for a moment while I gathered my wits.

"Answer me one question," I turned back to him. "The woman you killed, the store clerk, who was she to you?" I braced myself for another lie.

"She was my mother," he answered without hesitation.

I didn't speak to him again. I simply walked past him and out the front door. I walked swiftly down the sidewalk and around the corner to the police station, replaying the confession I'd secretly recorded on my phone as I walked. The streetlights glowed orange overhead. I walked closer and closer to the brick building and stopped when I saw my reflection in the full-length glass door. I looked tired, exhausted even. I needed to put all of this behind me. Was reporting Henry's transgressions the best way to move forward? What about my transgressions? I had felt doubt about Henry from the beginning and I ignored it on purpose. Yes, he took advantage of me, but I had enjoyed the ride for most of it. It wasn't his fault I was naive and broken too. We were both floundering back then and now here I was, twenty years later, pretending I didn't play a role in any of it. Yes, lies do breed lies, but secrets are the real tsunami. And Lord knows, after all these years, I still hadn't told a soul mine. The skeletons that hid in my closet were far worse than any Henry had locked away. If I walked through these glass doors now, I might as well be handcuffing myself.

I kept walking, past the police station, past the fire department, down Main Street, until I got to the park. Henry's bench was still there, no doubt replaced since we'd sat there many moons ago. I walked to it now and sat down. I stared out over the rippling ocean water and thought about all the times I'd done just this. The water always soothed my soul. This time, it didn't. Now I was more restless than I'd ever been. The choppy waves replicated my own emotions. The truth was, I'd done my best to forget, over the years, my sins that led to this very day. When I was a child, I'd blocked out the memory. Only recently, within the last few years, had I recovered my memory of that night long ago. The night that predicted my path for the rest of my life. Now that my parents were gone, I was alone with my secret. Or so I thought.

As I sat on the bench, soaking in the salty sea air, I could almost feel my little brother's limp body in my arms. I was four years old when my parents left me alone with Nate for just two minutes. My baby brother had been home from the hospital for a little while, a few months maybe, and all he ever did was cry. I remember hating him. I remember him being so loud. And then he wasn't loud anymore. I always blocked out what happened, never stopping to consider it in the slightest, until Derek and I went to see a friend's new baby a few years back. When I held their baby in my arms, I saw flashbacks of my baby brother, like a Deja vu moment. I brushed it off at the time but couldn't sleep after that. Finally, after weeks of frustrating sleepless nights, I went to see a hypnotist. After a series of sessions, I uncovered my responsibility for Nate's murder. And then it all made sense; my parents distancing themselves from me, moving out, moving on with a new life that didn't include me. I was practically grown before they adopted Susan. There they were, a sweet family, when I strolled in with Henry's gun, pretending to be the law that I should have been running from. I never got in trouble for Nate's death. I was four.

As I sat there on the park bench, suddenly a new memory unveiled itself. I was a young girl and I was standing between my parents. They were each holding one of my tiny hands. My mother was on my left, tears streaming down her face. My father was on my right, robustly shaking a police officer's hand.

"I won't say a word," the officer said, and his voice made my head spin. I knew that voice. It was…

"May I sit with you?" Henry stood to the side of my bench, interrupting my recollection.

"Sure," I said without looking at him.

He sat down but neither one of us spoke. The night grew darker, and the streetlights grew brighter. Finally, Henry broke the silence.

"Life is a crazy journey," he said. "There are many, many things I've messed up on."

"Were you ever a cop?" I looked evenly into his eyes.

"I was, for a while," he blinked.

"Then it was you." I clasped my hands together and laid them on my lap. Henry took a deep breath and exhaled slowly.

"I've always felt responsible for you, since that night." He reached over and took one of my hands in his. "I've never claimed to be a good person," he said. "I just…I really needed the money back then and your parents paid me generously to keep things quiet."

"They paid you?" I asked, swallowing hard.

"To look the other way. To keep you out of trouble, or themselves, I suppose."

"I was young. How could they..."

"You were four." He filled in the blanks. "And they were more concerned with their image than your mental health. They disappeared shortly after that, leaving you with the nanny. I was twenty-four. It was my first case. Not a day goes by that I don't wonder if I did the right thing. Everything could be so different."

"What do you mean?" My eyes stung as I listened to him.

"Maybe if we had gotten you the help you needed. Gotten you away from them. Investigated them. Maybe they would have been imprisoned and you would have been placed with a better family. A loving family. Maybe Catherine would still be alive. So many maybes."

"So, all of this is my fault," I summarized.

"No, that's not what I'm saying." He squeezed my hand. "I'm saying life is crazy and we can only do our best to navigate it. I did what I needed to do back then and it literally turned me into a psycho. I was always watching you. Always keeping tabs on you. My heart broke for you. For the lack of affection you received when Lord knows you deserved it all. I shouldn't have taken Richard's money that night."

"Well, I shouldn't have killed my baby brother." I stared out at the ocean. It was almost swallowed by the horizon now, as darkness settled around us.

"They shouldn't have left you alone with him," Henry stated. "Regardless, we can't live our lives based on shoulds or shouldn'ts. That's not how life works. We've both made colossal mistakes, me more so than you. You'll never know how sorry I am for everything." Just then, he got down on one knee in front of me. "Please, Ryan, let me spend the rest of my life making it up to you. Let me show you how much I love you and how much I've missed you. Please, Ryan, marry me." He pulled out a diamond ring and held it up in front of me.

I sat there, completely dumbstruck. Henry was nothing short of a sick and twisted man. His demons dug deep into his soul, and I knew this because mine matched his. After everything we'd been through, all the murders and lies and deceptions, he was still the only one I wanted to be with. A life with Henry was insanity played out on the big screen right in front of us, but a life without Henry was, well, empty.

I nodded at the man kneeling before me. The man who knew all my secrets and loved me anyway. The man who had brought me back to life not once, but twice. He'd rescued me from myself that Christmas Eve all those years ago, and now he was offering me a life of love and protection, a life that was sure to be nothing short of an incredible adventure. I was Henry's girl, and I had been since before I could even remember.

Is that silly, you wonder? To completely surrender to an addiction so sweet, so troubled, so reminiscent of yourself? Perhaps I should have been stronger and walked away, but it felt good to give in, to retreat almost, to stop worrying. When we got home, I stood in Suzie's doorway and looked at her room. I took a deep, calming breath, and crossed the threshold to clean up the mess I'd made earlier.

"We can throw all this stuff out," Henry appeared in the doorway behind me.

"No." My reaction surprised even me. I picked up the empty totes and stacked them back on top of each other in the closet, then I straightened the dresser drawers that I'd rummaged through.

"Ryan, it's fine," Henry rubbed my shoulders as I cleaned. "I'll toss all this stuff."

"No," I repeated myself. "She was real to me. Please, let's just leave this room alone." Tears threatened to cascade down my face. I took a deep breath and blinked them away.

"I'm sorry, Ryan," Henry apologized.

But how do you apologize for life? For secrets and lies all mangled together in fear. Fear of losing, fear of loving, fear of believing the truth. How do you apologize for being insecure, incapable, and inept at emotions? Does loving someone mean overlooking their flaws or wading in their world of mistakes, clinging to each other like lifeboats in a stormy sea? Henry and I were separately broken, but together we made sense. Together we were whole.

I slowly closed Suzie's door. I knew I'd never open it again like a chapter never to be reread. Henry grabbed us each a beer from the fridge, and we sat on the front steps together, knowing we were both finally home.

MORE BY MELISSA

Melissa also writes erotic romance
under the pen name Mel S.

<u>Demon Esha Trilogy</u>
DEMON ESHA
BECOMING ESHA
DESIRING ESHA

<u>EMBER</u>

www.ingramcontent.com/pod-product-compliance
Lightning Source LLC
LaVergne TN
LVHW041705060526
838201LV00043B/584